Love Unlimited

BY *At-Tariq* **The Comer by Night AKA** *GHOST*

Richmond Virginia

Love Unlimited
Copyright © 2024 by Larry Johnson

Website Againstalloddzpublicatons.com
againstalloddzpub@gmail.com

For distribution information and bulk ordering:
againstalloddzpub@gmail.com

Typesetting and interior designed by:
Against All Oddz Publications

DEDICATION

"More than 27 million people around the world endure the abhorrent abuse of human trafficking and forced labor, including thousands of people right here in the United States. Black girls and women are less likely to be seen as victims of gender-based violence, more likely to be hyper-sexualized, and are criminalized instead of offered support. It is a threat to global security, public safety, and human dignity." *Lets protect our girls...*

CHAPTER 1

The neighborhood was jumping with life as it normally did around this time of the day. At least three school buses were present, unleashing busloads of jubilant teenagers, anxious to return to their neighborhood. A crowd of students slowly bunch around two girls as the school bus disperse. They square up in the street to compete for a race. Ruby and Christal were the fastest in the neighborhood and perhaps the city. Many of the neighborhood kids were associated with the (RRHA) Richmond Redevelopment Housing Authority. Ruby and Christal were no exception.

The two of them matched up against some of the best talent in the city. The girls hadn't raced one another since grade school. Christal's mom had moved away for several years, but later decided to move back. Ruby could never beat Christal when they were little grasshoppers. Over the years, Christal would become a great source of Ruby's motivation. Ruby trained rigorously, in school, out of school, and out with friends... Get the picture, young Flo Joe was dedicated.

"GET READY, SET, GO!"

The vibrant neighborhood cheered as the duo bolted down the littered project streets. Children chased along side of them. Ruby had a slow start, but her walk down was relentless. To the right of her, Christal found Ruby there and was shocked, having to do a second look. They ran neck and neck. Ruby had violated Christal's space.

"GO FLO, you got her Ruby!"

"Don't let up Christal!!! Go! Go! Go!"

Pure pandemonium wreaked from the sideline. Then all at once, theirs an unexpected intrusion. A gold Cadillac Deville, whips the corner violently well above the speed limit. Ruby's mom, Linda walked outside, spotted the chaos and freaked out.

"RUBBBY! Out of the street! NOW GODDAMN IT! Get your butt in here. You too Christal!" Squad cars with blaring sirens were in hot pursuit of the vehicle. Ruby and Christal abandoned their race at Linda's demand as children ran for safety. Residents stood back cautious and clung to their children. More squad cars swarmed the neighborhood and surrounded the vehicle. The police had the main exits blocked off. Tucked between shabby project buildings, a few teenagers moved around suspiciously. They whispered and peeked their heads around the corner to steal a glimpse of the police action. They were four boys in all, minus Lil Jay. They were all underage.

The oldest being seventeen, they were shook. The cops had their friend cornered. On top of that, the boys were pressed hard by nearly every coke dealer that crossed their path. The drug pushers were especially livid. Heavy police presence brought their dope sales to a screeching halt. The Jack boys were expeditious, malicious even in the way they lifted cars from their victims. They had their own set of special skills, hot wiring a car within seconds. The driver was the moron of the group. His name was Lil Jay.

"I told that fool to get rid of that damn car," Cuddy, the leveled headed crew member complained. He had light skin complexion and chinky eyes with a solid and muscular build.

"He always wanna show off," Dennis adds.

"Now just look at where it got him." Cuddy says shaking his head. Big Diaz and a pack of thug figures walked up and cornered Cuddy and his boys.

"Look at where it got ya'll," Big Diaz corrected. He was a giant of a man with massive arms.

"I thought we told ya'll lil niggas to keep that hot shit out the projects," Kenny aggressively stated.

"Fucking up our money with this bullshit." Big Diaz had had enough of their antics. A third police cruiser drove by them.

Ruby's Apartment

An enormous photograph of Flo Jo was mounted on Ruby's bedroom wall. It was the infamous photo of the Olympic star proudly upholding the stars and stripes. The red, white and blue matched her tracksuit perfectly. The cherry red lipstick complimented her persona. It was Ruby's favorite picture of the Olympic star. Flo Jo was the fastest woman in the universe and undeniably gorgeous. Ruby wanted to be just like her. She had been training for the position most of her adolescent life. She loved to run, it gave her a sense of liberty. Whenever Ruby and Christal were together in her room, they would marvel at the giant portrait in admiration.

"Christal guess what?" Ruby raves ecstatic, rushing back to the room with quarter waters for them to drink.

"What?"

"You're lucky Lil Jay came when he did," Rudy teased and jerked her head to make her braids fly around to the front of her face. "Cause I was about to beat that ass." A burst of laughter from the girls.

"I can't even lie Ruby, you got fast girl. You surprised me. But beating me honey, I don't think so."

"To be continued, I guess." Ruby tipped her quarter water forward to meet Christal's. They put their drinks to their mouths and sipped.

"Hey, did Lil Jay look fine in that car or what?" Christal mentioned as an afterthought. Then she added, "he is sooo cute."

"Really Christal?" Are you talking about the stolen Cadillac or the police car?" Another hearty laugh from the girls.

CHAPTER 2

All roads lead to Armstrong High School. It was such a glorious day. The sun shinned with such brilliance. Ruby took in a breath of fresh air before walking onto the vast field with at least twenty of her team members. Finally, the day she had been training for arrived. Coaches and their athletes hit the field early to get a jump start on preparing for the competition. It was a huge day for the girls. Teams from all over the city were there to compete and show off their skills. Officials and volunteers arrived first to ensure that things ran according to plan. They're easy to spot, the volunteers wore green t-shirts with big white bold letters across the front that read *volunteer*. They moved faster than everyone else.

Every team had their own section to stretch and do drills. Meanwhile, the bleachers are filling up. The community never failed to support these events. People from all walks of life were arriving in droves. Ruby heard her supporters before she saw them. Her family was legendary for making grand entrances. "No weapon formed against you shall prosper child!" Linda chanted the minute she walked out on to the field.

Linda loved her bible verses. Ruby's aunt, little cousins and friends from the neighborhood all fill up their section of the bleachers. They wore t-shirts with Ruby's face on them. Others carried banners with her name and team number seventeen in bold. Ruby was uncomfortable when her family put her on the spot like that. The evil looks from teammates never went unnoticed. Many of them didn't have the support of their parents. She felt guilty in a sense. Even still, she wouldn't trade the love she got from her family in for nothing in the world.

Though separated, Ruby's dad, Roger never let her down. He was involved in every aspect of her life. Dad was there at every practice and track meet. Ruby waved at him taking his seat a few spaces over from Linda. Traffic cops had their work cut out for them today. Lines of cars stretched back for blocks. Folks and their children hiked on foot from nearby neighborhoods. Inpatient drivers honked their horns and cursed out jaywalkers.

"Asshole!!!" Kenny yells pissed. He abruptly stumped his brakes to prevent from hitting a sandy hair, white hippie who staggered clumsily out in front of their car. The hippie cuffed his skate board under his arm and flicked the impatient driver his middle finger. "Oh shit, did you see that dusty cracker?"

Big Diaz didn't reply. He said nothing for the next few seconds, but his disgust was duly noted. The narrow escape caused his cheesy pepperoni slice to smash into the car's dash board. They were already running late. Cars were barley moving due to the traffic jam. Big Diaz had more pressing business to attend to, and he didn't have the patience for Kenny's shit today. He instructed Kenny once the light changed to drop him off close to the school. A block or so later, the full-size Lexus coupe pulled to the side of the road. Passengers were jumping out of waiting cars and speedily making their way up to the packed event.

Big Diaz was up and out of the car fast. "Find somewhere to park," he yelled over his shoulder at Kenny as he hustled up to the school.

The first warnings from officials were blaring across the bullhorn for the athletes to report to their perspective places. Ruby was psyched up. Surrounded by teammates, she studied the potential threat from the opposition team. And every so often, she would cast a glance toward the bleachers where her family was seated. Christal noticed that Ruby appeared a tad bit distracted. Ruby glanced over at the bleachers again. "You good or what girl?" Christal asked. Her words brought a huge smile to Ruby's lips.

The girls were in the middle of stretching when Ruby's reply was drowned out by the announcements from the bullhorn. Officials were announcing the first alert to participants for the 400-meter dash. Christal could barely read Ruby's lips. Without warning, Ruby's eyes glow up like Christmas tree lights. Christal's piercing gaze danced back over to the bleachers. What could have her girl tripping so hard? Ruby was blushing from ear to ear.

Then it became clear when Cuddy and at least two of his boys entered the stadium. Many folks from the neighborhood acknowledged the boy's presence. Cuddy on the other hand only had eyes for Ruby. They noticed one another at the same time. Locked in a trance, the pair stood motionless. If as though for one faint second, they were the only two people present. Because of their age gap, Cuddy never spoke openly about his feelings for Ruby. Not even to his closest friends. The two had been crushing on one another for years now. The chemistry between the pair was potent and evident for all to see. When the time was right, they would certainly be together. He simply wanted Ruby to see him, and to know that he was there for her.

The officials were calling for participants to report to their designated places to prepare for the 400-meter dash. As if on cue, Ruby dotted over to the track. Recruiters from various schools and colleges were always there, lurking in the crowd. Speaking of recruiters, in a twisted sense, Big Diaz was something like a recruiter. Only he recruited for a different team and organization. Just like any other recruiter, he was there to scout out new prospects. It was best to get them while they were young and raise them up. Kenny walked up just in time to hear the gun blast and the racers take off like ferocious cheetahs. The crowd goes wild.

Big Diaz was already posted up, not far from where the recruiters and coaches were. He glanced over his shoulder and noticed Kenny there.

"It took you long enough, you almost missed my girl!" Big Diaz shouted over the excitement.

"Your girl??" Kenny uttered under his breath, cutting an eye over at Big Diaz confused.

"Just watch number seventeen! They say she like lightening boy," Big Diaz yells again. "Look at her go! She is walking her down nigga, do you see it, do you see her?" Big Diaz was ecstatic. He playfully grabbed Kenny's arm and shook him. Officials covered the race from the bullhorn. "Round of applause for, Ruby Parker!"

Ruby and Christal didn't compete in any of the races together. The duo dominated the rival teams and ranked first place in their perspective competitions. When it came time for the team to discuss the relay race, both girls expressed their desire to bring the baton home. Ruby and Christal felt they had earned the right to have their say. To settle the quarrel, coaches decided to have the winners compete in the 100-yard dash. There were at least a dozen more competitions and the 100-yard dash was one of them. This time, Ruby and Christal would be in the same race, which meant they'd finally face off. It was a secret pack between the team. The winner would bring home the baton. Ruby and Christal liked the sound of that.

CHAPTER 3

Ruby moved gracefully over to her starting block and focused on the track. She placed her feet inside the block and her fingers on the ground behind the starting line. Relaxing her muscles, her hands are slightly wider than shoulder width as she cast a quick glance over to her right at girls in similar stance. They were all ready, sniffing and scrutinizing their prey. They all wanted to be number one. But there could only be one. Ruby positioned her hips slightly above shoulder level. She pushed her feet hard into the blocks. Two lanes to her left, she caught Christal inspecting her. Their brief exchange last only seconds. Then there is the bang.

Ruby finished in first place, beating Christal by at least a few inches. The other girls didn't stand a chance. Ruby and Christal were unquestionably the fasted on their team. Ruby ran a perfect race, had she not, Christal would've capitalized and won the race instead. For years, Christal had been the star of their neighborhood. The one who everyone catered to and uplifted. She was the center of attention because of her unique athletic abilities. But arriving back home, it was a totally different feeling for Christal. It was the same movie, just a different character playing the part. And as much as she tried to mask her feelings, Christal was livid and took the lost hard. The quiet competition between the girls over the years was no secret. Christal was arrogant and loud, and felt the need to outdo Ruby at every turn. Ruby on the other hand, was a quiet assassin. She would never feed into Christal's antics. She trained and got better and faster, waiting for the day when she would finally shut Christal up. *Like today, and oh what a feeling.*

Whenever one of their own scored big, the neighborhood would all come together and throw a big party for the participants. It didn't matter what place the girls fell in, they were all winners and the people closest to them wanted to express it. The entire street was lit up with children playing fun neighborhood games. Linda put her giant Kent wood speaker on the front porch, and played good music for everyone to jam to. The grills were smoking hot and folks were filling their belly's and sipping on good drank. People who watched the race, stopped by Linda's to congratulate Ruby. She received gift cards, cash and plenty of well wishes. Because of the loud music and crowd, every so often a police cruiser would turn the corner and cruise by slowly to drive the dealers nuts. The street action was in full swing. Dealers boldly ran down on addicts in their cars looking to score drugs. Stashed in between a set of shabby buildings, dope pushers accepted cash in exchange for tiny clear bags of white substance. In every crack and cranny of the neighborhood, illegal sales were being made. But at the mere mention of the police presence, street dwellers scattered and ran for dear life like projects roaches when exposed to light.

CHAPTER 4

Katrina Watson

An adorable little girl points happily as one hundred balloons ascend to the air and drift off into the distant sky. Family and friends of Katrina Watson came together to hold a prayer vigil at the Martin Luther King Jr middle school. It was in walking distance from the neighborhood. The poor girl had been missing for one year today. And law enforcement were no closer to solving the case. Missing children were every parent's nightmare. There were many people present who loved Katrina. She simply disappeared without so much as a trace. And the track and field was her favorite place. Its also the location many of her peers last saw her. Not one shred of evidence or witness to give a clue or indication of where the lost child could be. It was especially frightening for the girls who Katrina schooled with and befriended throughout the years. No one had answers. No one knew a god damned thing! And it horrified the city. Parents were more cautious when it came to their children.

"On the count of three ya'll, WE LOVE YOU KATRINA!" One supporter chanted at the sea of bodies present as she stood firm with the family of Katrina Watson. "One, two, three... WE LOVE YOU KATRINA," Everyone chants simultaneously. Cuddy was next in line to hug Katrina's mom. He knew Katrina from school, and watched her blossom from a shy ponytail wearing little girl, into a cute outspoken teenager. It was always Katrina, Christal and Ruby. In the neighborhood and in school, they were the best of friends. Growing up, they would mimic three member, R&B girl groups, and have the best of fun. And then... *life happened*. Christal moved away. Ruby and Katrina stayed in contact, but Linda wasn't too fond of Katrina. Katrina had started moving fast, hanging around with unsavory people. Katrina suddenly dropped off the face of the earth. It was the strangest thing.

Cuddy was expressing his sympathy to Katrina's mother when he suddenly noticed Big Diaz over her shoulder twenty yards away. He stood in between the field goal, eying him in the most disturbing manner. Big Diaz had no expression, just a look of emptiness that unsettled him. A look that seemed out of place for such an event. Odd enough, Cuddy hadn't seen Big

Diaz since the encounter in the neighborhood. Cuddy's mind drifted into a blur at the mere sight of him.

"You right, we fucked up. But don't touch my boys. I'll take the beating... For all of them," Cuddy remarked just one week earlier.

Big Diaz and his boys had a hearty laugh at Cuddy's expense. But when Cuddy didn't budge, everyone took notice. *"Wait a minute,"* Big Diaz silenced everyone. *"This dude dead serious."* Shrugging his shoulders, Big Diaz turned to his boys.

"Well, tighten him up real fast. And hurry up so we can get back to this money." Cuddy is reminded of the beat down when Katrina's mom pressed against his injured ribcage a little too hard. The throbbing pain snapped, Cuddy out of his trance in time to see the big guy's massive arm motioning for him to come over. Cuddy eventually made his way over to Big Diaz and at least four of his guys. They were high off ganja, cracking up and flirting with every pretty face that walked by. Big Diaz smirked upon Cuddy standing in front of him.

"I like how you handled that situation the other night. You don't see too many young dudes with principals like that nowadays." Big Diaz said while examining Cuddy's swollen cheek. "Shit healing pretty good."

"Oh yeah, if you say so." Cuddy interjects. "Shit hurt like a mother fucker." Big Diaz laughs. Cuddy's boys kept their distance and avoided eye contact whenever Big Diaz looked their way. They were pretty pathetic, and Cuddy was noticeably embarrassed.

"You took one for the team. I respect that. Why don't you come and play for my team? Oh shit! Kenny look," Big Diaz tapped Kenny's shoulder.

"It's lucky number seventeen." Big Diaz becomes alive. No one around them knew what he meant. Before Cuddy realized it, Big Diaz was calling over a group of girls about to pass by them. One just happened to be Ruby. She was such a lovely girl. Brown skin bombshell with smooth ebony skin that highlighted her styled fishtail braids. Ruby's T-shirt had her team number seventeen on the front. They approached the guys. Cuddy is at Big Diaz's left and Kenny is on the opposite side. Another guy off in the distance moved around with his camera, snapping photos.

"Lucky number seventeen," Big Diaz says, causing Ruby to finally take notice of him. Big Diaz was so full of himself, that he couldn't see that the focused, track star only had eyes for Cuddy. Everyone knew of Big Diaz. It was no secret that he had a thing for younger girls. And when Ruby would see him in passing, he was always splurging his money around and talking louder than everyone else. He was a big showboat. But he'd never singled Ruby out before.

"Luck had nothing to do with it, trust," Ruby replies with a lovely smile, refocusing her attention to Cuddy. "Hi Cuddy," Ruby said finally. Cuddy's heart flushed. It had been some time since they were this close to one another, and the feeling was like electricity. They were face to face with everyone there, yet it was only the two of them.

"Hi Ruby." Cuddy says with a smile. "What's go- "Cuddy starts when Big Diaz rudely cuts in.

"Hey cutie, your number seventeen, right?"

"I...I am," Ruby reply's somewhat puzzled.

"Thought I recognized you." Big Diaz takes a wade of money out of his pocket and split a thousand between the girls with Ruby getting the bulk of the cash. Christal frowns and Ruby sees it. She had been acting funny ever since their race. Cuddy didn't say anything about the cash, he shrunk up like a prune instead. He didn't like another man giving his girl cash. He disliked the spark in Ruby's eyes at the sight of it. Even if it was an incentive for a job well done, Cuddy wasn't feeling it. Big Diaz made him feel small, and he loathed the feeling. Cuddy remained silent and masked his anger. Besides, it wasn't like Big Diaz knew about their thing.

14

CHAPTER 5

It was another uneventful drive out to the Marriott. The girls performing at Big Diaz's Birthday bash, had bused in from North Carolina, DC and Atlanta. Big Diaz kept the girls on ice until the big event. His extravagant birthday bash at Delightful Lounge was members only. These gentlemen had pockets that were as deep as the Nile river. The biggest criminals in the city were dropping in to be entertained by the exotic cuties. The last of the girls had come in on the greyhound this afternoon. Cuddy and Kenny were charged with the job of picking them up from the train station. They drove them to the hotel suite to settle them in with the rest of the girls.

It was Cuddy's second day on the gig and to be honest, he was quite impressed with the pay. They got the girls and fed the girls. Cuddy and Kenny looked after them on occasions while they worked. And for Cuddy's three days of dedicated work, he was paid a lumping two thousand. Low risk, high rewards was what Cuddy sought after. He figured catering to strippers was less risky, than stealing cars or pumping crack rock on a busy street corner. Plus, the work wasn't a walk in the park. They could be needy at times. Many of them appeared way too young to be hanging around people like Big Diaz and his hooligans. But everyone had to hustle and bustle to move forward in life. He wasn't about to knock theirs. And although he did a good job at masking his true feelings, something still ate at his conscious whenever he was in the girl's presence.

Truthfully, the job screwed with his peace of mind. Ruby would never approve of what he was doing to make money. And it almost felt like a violation of their sacred bond. But he had a plan. Big Diaz gave him an opportunity, and Cuddy would use it to come up and create his own lane. Cuddy promised himself to never allow Big Diaz, or anyone else for that matter, to make him feel the humiliation he felt that day at the track meet. The way Ruby reacted to all that doe being shoved in her face made him sick. No man would ever show him up that way again. He promised. Cuddy did his job to the letter, and often got slack from the fellas for never unwinding and enjoying himself. Surrounded by temptation, but he never cracked under the pressure. Lover boy was head over heels in-love with Ruby. It was that affection for his rare jewel, that kept his lust at bay. She was all Cuddy wanted.

The last girl was on stage finishing up. Belle was the hottest dancer of them all. She had an amazing physic and was skilled in the erotic way that she danced. But her greatest talent was her exciting pole performance. The final show was always a packed house. They made the place rain with cash whenever Belle hit the stage.

It was a great night for Big Diaz's pockets. He and his entourage were outside Delightful Lounge, packing the girls into the Sprinter vans. Girls were not allowed to speak to anyone during this time. Not even customers they earlier entertained. Big Diaz ran a tight shift and was very protective of the females, especially on the last night when it was time to get them back. Cuddy was not allowed to go beyond that point. He helped get the girls ready to go, but that was as far as he went, which struck him as odd.

Right before he assisted the last girl inside the van, she held the door shut to prevent Cuddy from opening it. Cuddy didn't recognize her outside of her performance attire, but he remembered her face. The dancer appeared alarmed to the sense of threat. She was quiet for a moment while cautiously casing the parking lot. She focused her attention back on Cuddy once Big Diaz and Kenny walked back inside the club.

"Do you know what happened to my cousin?" She blurts out. "She was at the first party, do you remember?" Her words were fast and falling all over one another. "You told us it was your first day working." Cuddy was reluctant to respond, but he recognized her. She kept teasing him that night and calling him a fag, because he wouldn't accept the lap dance she offered. She flirted with Cuddy every chance she got. But Cuddy wasn't clear on what the frantic girl meant. And more importantly, what was it with the urgency in her face? It felt like a scene straight out of a horror flick. Her horrifying eyes and the look of desperation, freaked Cuddy out. Belle struggled to keep it together. "Dazzie, she's missing. Three girls never made it back that night, including my cousin, Dazzie. "Do you know what's happening here-?"

"Hey!" Big Diaz's bark was like a mighty bolt of lightning. Everyone stopped and stood motionless like mannequins. Cuddy wanted to let the girl know that he had no idea where her people was, or what she was insinuating. He was totally clueless. When the dancer failed to move in a hastily manner, Big Diaz yelled, ***get the fuck in the truck bitch!*** The dancer flinched at the harsh command. Cuddy was even shocked at the boss's choice of words. How long had he been there? Up until now, the girls had never been disrespected that way. Big Diaz had choice words for anyone who got out of line with his girls, so his response was unexpected. Belle climbed inside the van but never took her sight away from Cuddy. The van's door slammed in her face, leaving Cuddy horrified. What had just happened? He had this eerie feeling inside as he started his stride over to the club where Big Diaz and Kenny waited. Cuddy was drilled by them both.

"What did that bitch say to you?" The giant hovered over Cuddy like a lofty mountain.

"I don't know mane, bitch was rushing. She wanted to know what was taking ya'll so long. Fuck was I supposed to do, not talk to her?"

"That's exactly what you supposed to do." There was a sinister look about him that baffled Cuddy. He hesitated for a brief second, surprisingly caught off guard. Big Diaz had never come at him so strong. He shook off his gloom and replied. "Say less my nigga, I got it."

Satisfied with Cuddy's answer, the guys took off in a hurry without saying a word, sprinter van's in tow. Cuddy stayed back with the club members to help clean up. Felisha was a cook. Within seconds of Big Diaz leaving, she rushed up to Cuddy with a nervous look that caused the boy's heart to skip a beat.

"Unh-uh," she shoved a black duffel bag into Cuddy's chest. "Here you go honey, them high ass niggas left this behind the bar. I want no parts of that shit." Felisha walked off in the opposite direction before Cuddy could protest. For a second, he was uncertain of his next move. Then he noticed the extremely bright neon restroom sign. Suddenly, he had to use it.

CHAPTER 6

On The Road

Panic settles on Big Diaz face as he cut an eye over at Kenny. He lowers the volume on the stereo, giving Big Diaz a look. "What is it?"

"I fucked up. The duffel bag my nigga, tell me you grabbed it." The SUV comes to a screeching halt at the corner of Broad Street and Boulevard Avenue. The unexpected stop nearly caused the tailing SUV to collide into the back of them.

Kenny turned to Big Diaz saying, "I don't because you had it." Kenny shakes his head in distress, pounding the steering wheel in alarm. "You put it behind the bar when you went to check on Cuddy." Vehicles behind them are sounding their horns and yelling at the entourage of SUV's and Sprinter van's holding up traffic. Unbothered by the loud raucous, Big Diaz played the whole scene back in his head. The cook who alerted him to Cuddy and the stripper talking outside the night club. He tucked his bag behind the bar to go and check on Cuddy. Big Diaz's somber expression revealed his displeasure. "Turn this bitch around!"

Delightful Lounge

Just about everyone had left except for a few employees. The place had been cleaned. A few minutes earlier, Felisha served Cuddy chicken wings, fries and a large half lemonade and iced tea. He was halfway through his meal when he heard commotion outside. A car door slammed shut. And then Big Diaz walked in with Kenny on his heels. Felisha was there to meet them. Cuddy observed the exchange between them from his booth in the far corner. He peered down at the duffel bag next to him at the exact same time Felisha was pointing them in his direction. Big Diaz examined the duffel bag as he approached Cuddy's booth, giving Cuddy a long hard stare. Kenny took a wingding from Cuddy's plate and bit it while Big Diaz scooped up the duffel bag. He unzipped the bag, peeked inside and filled around. "Did you take your pay out here yet?"

The question caught Cuddy by surprise. Big Diaz was feeling him out. He wanted to know had Cuddy poked his nose where it didn't belong.

"I wouldn't do that without your permission," Cuddy answers finally and doesn't bat an eye. "But now that you here, I could definitely use that paper." Big Diaz smiled for the first time since he arrived. "Sure my nigga," Big Diaz takes a few stacks of cash from his bag and hands it to Cuddy. "You did good tonight, there's a tip in there for you too."

"Good looking out," Cuddy remarks before taking another bite off a wingding.

"Come on, we gotta get these girls to the bus station." Kenny says. "We can drop you off afterwards.

CHAPTER 7

The streets are slowly filling with children who leave their homes to walk up to their perspective bus stops for school. Cuddy stands across the street from Ruby's bus stop. Ruby and Christal walked out of their apartments at the same time and started up toward their bus stop. A trucks engine roars. The black company van, parked inconspicuously at the corner of Rosetta street beside an abandon house on the corner goes unnoticed. The occupants inside, smiled joyously at children who waved at them on their way to the bus stop. The van cruises slowly as Ruby and Christal crosses the street to say hi to Cuddy before their bus came. Cuddy and Ruby were nearly twenty feet apart when that same van stopped in front of them. The sliding doors flew open in a horrifying manner.

Christal was so shaken, that she pivoted and dashed off in the opposite direction. Ruby never saw it coming. The track star is abducted right in front of Cuddy, and there wasn't a thing he could do. He clammed up, and for a few dismal seconds, he felt immobilized. The neighborhood residents ducked behind window blinds before opening their doors. Cuddy was scrutinized by them all as they stepped out onto their porches in union. Then they charged at him.

"Cuddy! Wake up boy! Your soaking wet honey. I made breakfast." Auntie Barbra turned up her nose at Cuddy's damp t-shirt saying, "make sure you wash up first."

"Alright, I'm up auntie. Give me a sec."

"Another one of those dreams hunh? Dang boy, what type of demons you got chasing you?" Cuddy's aunt Barbra remarked while standing over him burning sage.

"Cut it out auntie." Cuddy laughs.

He finally sat up in bed after his aunt left the room. His appetite was off and he picked over his pancakes at the breakfast table. The girls from Delightful Lounge was still in his head. He couldn't shake it. Things weren't the same for Cuddy since Big Diaz's party.

He wasn't totally honest with Big Diaz about the duffel bag. Perhaps

Cuddy had bitten off a little more than he could chew. The duffel bag of course contained well over 100k. But it wasn't the cash that aroused intense interest, causing Cuddy's flesh to crawl. It was something a lot more sinister. Had Cuddy opened Pandora's box?

Unearthed under the cash, was a black composition notebook with a detailed price list for organ harvesting. Cuddy had no idea such an underworld existed. There were hundreds of pictures of underage girls, including snap shots of Rudy. His heart sunk. Ruby had over a dozen photos from several angles, taken the day of the track meet. Cuddy thought of the guy with Big Diaz, snapping pictures that day. The more Cuddy leafed through photos of Ruby, the more his heart burned. The more violent his blood boiled. Why were there so many photos of Ruby? The more he searched, the more stunned Cuddy became. He stumbled up on Katrina Watson's photo. And another with Katrina, Christal and Ruby from over two years earlier at their bus stop. Perhaps this was the first.

Big Diaz at Katrina's vigil the other day was a major red flag. The pieces were falling into place, and it horrified him. Was Delightful Lounge just a front for something more disturbing? Snatching black girls and selling them *And Big Diaz's club was there recruiting station?* Cuddy thought at least. He didn't know for sure. But still, with all that Cuddy thought he knew, nothing in the world could've prepared him for Belle's demise. The frighten dancer who approached him, was found dead on the train from an alleged Fentanyl overdose. It crushed Cuddy to the core to watch the girl's family speak of their tragedy. He didn't know what to do. How long before law enforcement connected the missing girls to Big Diaz and his slaughterhouse? Or Cuddy even? Belle's cousin Dazzie was presumed still missing, and Belle suddenly turns up dead? With the photos found of Ruby, coupled with Big Diaz's behavior at the track meet, it was safe to say that Ruby could be next. And Cuddy couldn't allow that to happen. He had to protect Ruby at all cost. Things just got real.

CHAPTER 8

The only draw back from such a job, was the way that it screwed with his conscious. He needed to build some quick capital and fast. Things were happening. Cuddy had been promoted and given more access to Big Diaz's enterprise. It was a covert sex trafficking business passed off as a chain of strip clubs. Secretly, they funneled girls through the business with the belief that they'd dance, make lots of money only to be discarded of and never heard from again. Like Dazzie and Belle, hundreds of girls came through the pipeline monthly. A stunned Cuddy was oblivious to the existence of such a market. And it weighed heavily on him to be a part of it. Big Diaz and his kind were a cancer to the community. The city's daughters were not safe, especially his Ruby.

Business aside, Cuddy didn't take kindly to Ruby being a part of Big Diaz's portfolio. The nerve of that bastard to smile in his face knowing the circumstances. But Cuddy had to play it smart. He needed to stay close to Big Diaz, and on the inside just in case Ruby was taken. At last, Ruby was in his eyesight. Cuddy had her meet him a couple blocks from the neighborhood at the city park. They hadn't seen one another since Katrina's vigil, and he knew she had choice words for him. He sat alone on the bench overlooking the vast city, thinking of beauty and the beast. Cuddy wondered with all the city's beauty and immaculate structures, how could it saturate so much bestiality.

His head was about to explode. He had a lot to drop on Ruby and he didn't know where to begin or how much to reveal to her. Cuddy had prolonged seeing Ruby for as long as he could, but he couldn't afford the luxury of keeping her in the dark any longer. It was difficult to face her while he worked for Big Diaz. But here she was as lovely as ever. Ruby fell into Cuddy's arms as if she'd been longing to be held by him. Cuddy planted kisses all over her forehead, face and finally her luscious full lips. He whispered to her, "babe, I missed you so much." Then without warning, comes a voice over the handheld device inside a shirt pocket on the bench beside them. "You got the package? Over."

Ruby gawks over at the bench, and subsequently at Cuddy in astonishment. She slowly backed out of his arms as Cuddy grabbed the device from the bench and spoke into it.

"I got her, over."

"What the fuck," was Ruby's reply. She was alarmed. Her horrifying eyes canvased the entire area. Her head shifted from left to right with breakneck speed. Cuddy saw her reaction and immediately took her hands, pressing them up against his lips. He gazed into her terrified eyes. "I know this looks crazy, but it's not like that. I would die for you. Do you believe me?"

"I do Cuddy…" Ruby's heart was thumping and all she could think of was the moments before Katrina's abduction. Did she have a fighting chance? At any rate, Ruby wasn't about to make the same mistake. She watched every passing car. She scrutinized every strange face.

"Ruby, you are good." Cuddy reassured her.

"I haven't seen or heard a word from you in months. You have me come here and I find this? Everything about this meeting is suspect to me." Ruby was suspicious and skeptical of Cuddy at this point. "What's going on? Tell me now… or I'll scream nigga!"

Ruby's ice cold glare cuts Cuddy like a knife. "Oh shit, babe chill." Cuddy chokes back a laugh. Ruby's eyes were alarming and he could see that she was shaken. Cuddy had rehearsed this moment a thousand times in his head and somehow, he still managed to screw it up. She was about to break, and he saw it. "I think I know what happen to Katrina," he said suddenly.

"Wait, what?!" Ruby remarked dumbfounded. *Had this nigga been reading my mind?*

"Just listen, Ruby," Cuddy stops her. "Please. That was Lil Jay's voice you heard over the radio."

"Lil Jay is locked up," Ruby states confidently.

"He's out, and he's keeping an eye on things for me."

"An eye on things? What exactly does that mean? Am I in danger or something?" Ruby pressed Cuddy hard.

"Sit down, and I'll tell you everything," Cuddy suggested, gesturing for her to reclaim her seat. Ruby did another scan of the area. There was a mother with a kid by the swings. Two guys, one older than the other, walked by on the street. The older gentlemen briefly looked their way, but kept moving along. Ruby wasn't convinced, making Cuddy confirm Lil Jay's identity over the device before cautiously taking her seat. Cuddy pulled a portrait from his front shirt pocket, scrutinizing it a few seconds before finally handing the photo to Ruby. Cuddy saw the confusion on her face. "I don't understand, who took this photo of me? And why do you have it?"

"Listen babe." Cuddy's eyes turned into tiny black beads, cold and relentless, horrifying Ruby. It was a far cry from his normal demeanor. "I can get killed for what I'm about to say. You can't say a word to anyone, not even your mama…Do you understand? At least for now." Ruby slowly nods her head in agreement.

26

CHAPTER 9

"Lucky number seventeen," Ruby utters bitterly under her breath while folding up fresh linen with her mom in the living room. Linda could sense that Ruby was not her self. Her dad even noticed her gloom when he dropped by earlier today to check on her. Mom and dad laid off after, Ruby assured them that she was okay. Ruby admitted that she had seen Katrina's mom today, and that it made her think of Katrina. **Ruby lied.** She'd rather tell Linda anything but the truth, so a lie would have to suffice for now.

Cuddy was perfectly clear on the importance of total silence. But lose lips nearly sunk the ship when her ace, Christal dropped by unexpectedly. Like everyone else, Christal could sense her low vibration. Ruby for one split second, pondered the idea of confiding in Christal. But out of nowhere, Cuddy's stark warning, boomed in her head like a big tin drum. Christal was sweet, talkative, and bad at keeping secrets. News as spicy as this, the babble mouth teen would never shut up about. Instead, Ruby simply reiterated the same lie she told her parents. That speaking to Katrina's mom today upset her and put her in a bad head space.

Christal did something unexpected. She apologized for being a bitch the last couple of weeks. She even confessed to being jealous of Ruby's win, asking for forgiveness. Ruby accepted her apology, and then Christal invited Ruby to come out with her to a party. It had been ages since the girls had hung out. Ruby couldn't seem to stay focus after the meeting with Cuddy. Part of her felt guilty knowing what she knew. Not even one month ago, the neighborhood united to show that Katrina hadn't been forgotten. Katrina was her childhood friend, and here she was doing absolutely nothing with the information she knew. She found the number to the National Human Trafficking Hot line. She wanted to do the human thing. But revealing Cuddy's information prematurely could prove fatal. Of course Ruby wanted to help her friend, however, she just wasn't prepared to die for it.

There was never a dull night out with Christal. Unfortunately though, Ruby declined Christal's invitation to hang out. Instead, what she wanted to do was warn her girl that she could possibly be a target. Ruby needed to tell her to protect herself, and to trust no one. But sadly, all Ruby did was watch Christal leave unguarded, and totally unaware of the hidden dangers ahead. Ruby felt horrible and questioned her loyalty to her friends. Whatever plan Cuddy was cooking up, it needed to be done with and fast. She didn't know how long she could keep a lid on. Her nerves were off the Richter scale. She was now critical of the guys in the neighborhood she'd known most of her life. The block huggers and gangsters who smiled at her daily, gave her money and watched her grow up. But who were they really? If they could steal, kill and deal poison to their own, weren't they capable of something atrocious as sex trafficking? The selling of their own peers and oftentimes family members. It was all for the love of money, right? The hearts of men, were filled with betrayal and sin. She thought of the day of the track meet and afterwards, Katrina's vigil.

Everything that glittered sure wasn't gold. Big Diaz's smile and cash offering, was like that of a serpent trying to deceive. Ruby was being baited into what she now realizes, was a plot against her life. This was no time to fool herself. Katrina had been taken. And what Cuddy revealed to her, was absolutely inconceivable. In a sense, Ruby felt like she was living on borrowed time. When would the body snatchers come for her or Christal? Would the girls be picked off one by one? She adored Cuddy and wanted to believe wholeheartedly that their feelings were mutual. Later, she began to wonder about the extent of Cuddy's involvement. Was all the other girl's fair game except for Ruby? Could she really trust Cuddy with her life? She hated keeping the one person in the dark, who's advice she desperately needed right now.

She knew mom all too well. Linda would blow the lid off. What a weighty burden to lay on a person. With Cuddy and his extracurricular activities, he was certainly the last person in the world that Ruby should be around. Nevertheless, Cuddy was the only person she wanted to be around. She had been saving herself for him. And just the thought of him working around so many nude girls, didn't agree with her spirit. Ever since their meeting, she had been longing to be back in his arms.

CHAPTER 10

Days pass without a word from Cuddy, and Ruby's having a hard time concentrating in class. When one of the teacher's top students show decline for no apparent reason, a dedicated teacher will take notice. And so it was with Ruby. While students prepared for the bell to ring, Ruby appeared to have misplaced something. Usually around this time, the teacher is moving around, cleaning up for her next class. Today, she sits quietly behind her desk observing her students, one student in particular.

The bell sounded. An impatient Ruby was now frantically searching through her backpack, discreetly canvasing the floor area around her desk. Every so often, she would gaze up to catch, Ms. Battle scrutinizing her. Students are bailing for the door and finally after minutes of an unsuccessful search, Ruby hurriedly push everything back inside her book bag. She tosses it over her shoulder, and was ready to rush to the door where Christal waited outside. Ms. Battle called her back. "What..." Ruby uttered in disbelief. *'A fine time to call me, this is bullshit!'* Ruby hissed under her breath.

"Yes Ms. Battle."

"You can close the door." Ms. Battle remarked sternly, which struck Ruby as odd. Ms. Battle was the nicest person ever, but the teacher's vibe today threw Ruby for a loop. Ruby closed the door in the middle of Christal's protest. Ruby shrugged her shoulders hopelessly at Christal before slowly turning around. Ms. Battle waved a sharp object at her like a magic wand. She was a fair skin, African American woman in her mid-thirties. Ruby thought she had the prettiest set of pearl white, even teeth she'd ever seen. Ms. Battle smiled easily at Ruby as the bashful girl took the empty seat across from her.

"I noticed you looking for something. Would it happen to be this?" When Ruby doesn't reply, the teacher goes on to say, "I saw it fall out of your book bag, Ruby. Now, do you want to go home, or do you want to go to the principal's office? Give me one good reason why I shouldn't just march you straight there." Ms. Battle was firm. "Your mom can't know about this. Did someone give this to you?" Ms. Battle was baffled at Ruby's actions.

There was suddenly a look of defeat on Ruby's face. She sits up straight in her seat and twist uncomfortably. Clearing her throat, she asks, "have you watched the news lately Ms. Battle?" Ruby stops the teacher as she struggles to reply. "You don't have to answer that," Ruby says with a faint smile. "There are 100,000 victims of human trafficking worldwide. Over half of that number are young black girls like me. In our city alone, in the last year, over seven girls have been reported missing, including my best friend. No one gave me the blade Ms. Battle. Katrina was snatched last year. And last month, we had her one-year anniversary. This is real for me... Katrina last year, I could be taken this year."

"Oh my God, Ruby. You mustn't speak that way." Ms. Battle remarked appalled.

"But it's my reality Ms. Battle. So yes, I carry that for protection because to be honest, I'm afraid for my life."

Ms. Battle doesn't respond right off. Ruby's harsh truth leaves her in stunned silence. She taught Katrina for two years. The teacher got to witness first-hand how close they were. To now look around her classroom and see Katrina's seat empty, or occupied by another student, was heart-wrenching. Ms. Battle could sympathize with Ruby's reasoning. Initially, the teacher had every intention to personally take Ruby up to the principal's office and have her properly dealt with. But Ruby was right. The statistics didn't lie. Ruby was a target, along with every other melanated girl who looked like her. Ms. Battle struggled with her emotions.

"I understand... I do. But the school and its regulations are a different story. You can get in serious trouble for this, Ruby." Ms. Battle's compassionate eyes danced around undecided as she twirled the blade in her hand. "And I don't want that for you. Don't expect to get this back." The teacher smiles and winks her eye. "And don't worry, I won't snitch you out, it'll be our little secret."

A burst of relief spreads across Ruby's face. The roar of bus engines drew their attention to the window simultaneously. Ruby's bus was pulling away. Ms. Battle saw the panic in Ruby's face and quickly eased her fears. "Don't worry, I'm your designated driver for today. Give me a second to finish up here, and I'll drop you off. How's that sound?"

"Like a plan, Ms. Battle," Ruby replied so relieved that she jumped to her feet and helped the teacher clean up the classroom.

CHAPTER 11

Cuddy's crew oftentimes stole high performance vehicles for the operation to assist in moving the girls around from time to time. It happened by accident really. One of the truck's filled with girls had an engine issue. It was severe enough to break down on the highway one early morning after a long night. The girls were exhausted, and needed to rest up for their next show the following day. And most importantly, being on the highway at such an hour, wasn't a good look for them at all. Big Diaz and his cronies were in a panic, fearing the cops might come and find them this way. Big Diaz couldn't locate an extra vehicle at that hour. Cuddy just happened to be working that night. He was riding along in the second vehicle with more girls. He assessed the problem and instantly knew what to do.

Many of the girls were possibly underage. Cuddy, like a savior made one call and in a matter of minutes, had Lil Jay drive up in an almost identical Sports Utility Vehicle. Big Diaz was impressed to say the least. He didn't understand how Cuddy was able to make it happen so expeditiously. He didn't care either. Relieved, the girls all filled the truck and was able to make it back to their hotel without incident.

Delightful Lounge
A man sits in a dimly lit conference room with a digital camera on the table near him, and equipment that took up a third of the table. He takes long hard tokes from his cigarette while skimming through photos of underage ebony flavored girls. The girl on a particular set of pictures, he paid close attention to. He counted her photos repeatedly and still seemed to be dissatisfied. Big Diaz and Kenny walked in. Big Diaz's attention is immediately drawn to the newspaper article on the table. He walked over to plop down in one of the empty seats around the table. Across from him, the front page of the Times Weekly read, ***"64,000 Missing Black Women and girls in the United States and No one Seems to Care."***

"Why the fuck is this here?" Big Diaz says, grabbing the article from the table. He gaze at it for a moment before tossing it to Kenny. "Get that shit out of my eyesight!"

"It's only information. Don't go getting all sentimental on me," says the camera guy whose name happened to be Mark. "Gotta run something by you."

"Bro, you gotta relax. Is it about that bag again?"

"I specifically packed the bag in a certain order. And it wasn't the way I left it. Photos are missing. Why do I know this? It's the very first photo I took of her. Ruby. Your boy Cuddy was alone with the bag. How much do you trust him? What if he took the photo to show his girl as proof? Do you see where I'm going with this?"

"Do you think I'm a fool? I got him working for me for a reason. I got a tail on the little bitch! I think you need to stick to snapping photos and allow me to take care of the business.

"Diaz, don't make the mistake and think that you are bigger than the organization you work for. That we both work for. And snapping photos... it's just one of the jobs I do. It happens to be my least favorite. I could be camera man today. Or gun man tomorrow. Just depends on the circumstances." The room falls silent as Kenny and Big Diaz exchange questionable looks of concern. Kenny speaks in an effort to restore order. The tension was thick in the room.

"Relax cameraman, we're keeping a close eye on her."

"Let's get one thing straight." The defiant guy stood for the first time with his attention directed at Kenny. "I'm not your fucking camera man here to take photos," Mark barks. He faced Big Diaz. "They want Ruby! I suggest you stop fucking around."

"Or what, "Big Diaz said, jumping from his chair to stand face to face with Mark. Big Diaz knew the organization had far reach, but he wasn't about to allow this puny sucker to say another word. "OR WHAT!"

"Or perhaps the organization will employ me for the job that I'm really good at." Big Diaz and Mark face off like raging pit bulls. No one had ever threatened Big Diaz that way and live to talk about it. But he had never made so much cash. Big Diaz was now a part of something much bigger than himself. And so, he had to yield to a higher hierarchy.

CHAPTER 12

Barbra had sought custody of Cuddy at the tender age of six years old. Cuddy's mom was murdered in the same neighborhood he grew up in. She was a stone cold addict whose dealer she'd stolen drugs from one times too many. She ripped him off in the past, but sadly, the enraged dealer went el loco on this day. Auntie did a good thing by stepping in for her sister and gaining guardianship of her nephew. Cuddy never talked about his mom. It's like he totally blocked her out of his head. No tears, no need for comfort, perhaps he suffered from dissociative amnesia. Auntie worried about Cuddy not grieving his mom's death. The way Cuddy dealt with her absence, was by not dealing with it. If that made any sense at all.

Ruby did everything with her friends. Today, they skipped class. Ruby was more disciplined than her peers. She didn't drink or smoke joints, unlike Christal and the others. Cuddy was the drug of her choice. When she couldn't get him, she 'd have withdrawals. Ruby didn't do things just for the sake of doing them. Skipping class for her, was a means for her and Cuddy to link up.

The small group were just a block away from the park to puff their ganja when a clean Cadillac drove up along side of them. Ruby cautiously inched backwards toward the curb. Christal, Robby and Dallas were a few feet ahead. Before she could catch up with her friends, the driver honked the horn. She heard, "its Lil Jay, Ruby. I'm here for Cuddy." His statement brought her to a halt. She alerted her friends. "Its Lil Jay ya'll," Ruby hollered over her shoulder before approaching the car.

"You ready? Hop in." Ruby stood back with her hand on her hip, inspecting the practically brand new car. It was clean, inside and out. She laughed. "I'm not getting in no car with you fool. Is this stolen?"

"No," Lil Jay replied offended. He gestured to the keys in the ignition. "Does it look stolen?" He cracked a smile. "The game done changed, baby girl. A nigga don't steal cars no more."

"Unh un, Ruby!!" Christal hollers back. Robby and Dallas only wanted to smoke weed. If Ruby returned before they had to be back at school, the boys could care less. They were more excited about Lil Jay's car. Just last year, they were all hanging and skipping class, and now to see Lil Jay whipping a car that wasn't stolen was a step up.

"Ain't like you got a lot of time," Lil Jay remarked, drawing Ruby's undivided attention. "And ol boy expecting to see you." Ruby stood undecided, but only for a few seconds. Giving his history, Ruby wasn't at all excited to catch a ride with Lil Jay. But under no circumstances, was she going to miss a meeting with Cuddy. She needed answers that only he could give. She didn't know how long she could keep Linda at bay. Mom could sense something off with her daughter, beginning to press Ruby more and more each day. Just the other day, Linda caught Ruby in a deep trance.

"You know I'm here for you if you ever need to talk, okay sweetheart," mom reassured her daughter. Then she made Ruby stand to examine her further, hugging Ruby in the most gentle manner. Ruby smiles while reflecting over her mom and how wonderful she was. Every so often, she'd cast a nervous glance in the rear view as Lil Jay drove in silence. He bobbed his head to sounds from the factory stereo. Ruby couldn't hide her excitement.

CHAPTER 13

The black Chevy Buick cargo van circled the block twice already. Exerting pressure but staying at a safe distance, there was no room for error. The head honchos of the illicit organization clamped down. A circle of trust between heartless men. The golden opportunity attributed to their employees, removed their conscious of the heinous act. Girls were bought, sold and shipped like cargo, having to surrender to many ungodly acts. Never to be seen or heard from again. Others were dismembered and their organs sold to the highest bidder. Inside the transport vehicle, the men held the lowest position on the totem pole. There only duty was to snatch and deliver.

Draped in blue overalls with visible company logos on their front shirt pockets, they moved stealth like. Robby and Dallas are none the wiser. They're both taken down and overpowered by blue overalls. A third guy ejected from the van's side door, moving with skilled precision. Christal's adduction was precise. She was snatched and thrown headfirst inside the back of a moving van that sped away.

The petite sized ebony woman with dreads that reached her backside, lived in a house across from the park. She heard the burning rubber, but could barely make out what she was witnessing. When the smoke cleared, she noticed what appeared to be endangered kids. The boys were stunned. Within seconds, she had rushed across the street to aid them. Dallas managed to say, "call the police please, ma'am! They took our friend!"

"Who took your friend, sweetheart?" She was confused and terrified all at once.

"It was a black van. Two men, they took us down hard," Robby utters through agonizing pain. He had a nasty, open gash on the top of his forehead that leaked triplets of blood.

"Yes, I saw a black something speeding away!" She was already dialing into her phone. The boys were lost and confused, and didn't have a clue what had just transpired. This was so bad. They were already skipping school and smoking weed, and this happens. The boys had a lot of explaining to do. They wanted to bail before the cops arrived, but couldn't find the nerve to abandon their friend that way. A new reality was about to set in for Robby and Dallas. Christal was gone. The cops would be looking for witnesses that could help them with any leads to locate Christal's where abouts.

CHAPTER 14

He tried to make the place spotless. Auntie Barbra was gone until tomorrow, so there was only a small window for him to see Ruby. Cuddy rushed to the window at the sound of a car's engine out front and a door slamming shut. It was Ruby, hopping out of Lil Jay's ride. She was so lovely, that Cuddy could only stand there momentarily mesmerized. He quickly dashed to the door to let her in. Lil Jay is backing out of the circular driveway as Cuddy stood aside while Ruby planted a juicy kiss on his cheek before walking in.

The pair are laughing up a storm when the phone rings next to them on the coffee table. They're snuggled up in the cozy living room in front of the tub, watching comedy central. Lil Jay is on the line and he's ecstatic. Cuddy and Lil Jay spend a short while on the phone and afterwards, Cuddy hangs up, and doesn't say anything. His silence is telling and Ruby senses the ill vibe instantly.

"You haven't said a word since you hung up, who was that?" When Cuddy doesn't reply, Ruby sat up and faces him. Cuddy's blank stare concerns Ruby. "What is it, is something wrong?"

"This shit is really going down," Cuddy utters to no one as he finally snaps out of it, focusing his attention on Ruby. "Babe, try not to freak out. I got some serious shit to lay on you about Christal." Cuddy sighs.

"What the fuck Cuddy?" Ruby was impatient.

"They took Christal babe."

"WHAT! Don't fuck around like that."

Ruby didn't want to believe what she was hearing. Her worst fears had come true. The panic in her gut was tremendous, and it felt like every organ in her body shifted. Ruby's mind drifts back to her meeting with Ms. Battle, and her stubbornly sitting across from her teacher. ***This is real for me… Katrina last year, I could be taken this year.*** Ruby expressed the sentiment to her teacher not even two weeks ago. And now Christal was gone. Ruby felt unsafe and unsure of whether the kidnappers saw her there at the park.

If Cuddy hadn't sent for Ruby when he did, perhaps it would be her instead of Christal. Did Cuddy know this would happen? Was Lil Jay her night and shining armor? There to sweep her away in the nick of time? Ruby couldn't be a naive fool in this hour. She needed to lay the news on her mom, and then she would know what to do from there. She couldn't think straight. There were so many emotions flowing. Ruby felt ashamed, guilty even for not telling her friend that her life was in danger. First Katrina, and now Christal, how could this happen again? ***How did I let you talk me into keeping silent about this? This is your fault. If I had called the police when I had the chance, Christal would still be here.*** Lord knows, Ruby wanted to scream in Cuddy's face. Instead, she simply went blank.

"Ruby, are you good," a concerned Cuddy asked.

"I'm not Cuddy. I feel sick and dirty. I gotta call the police. My mama, or somebody because this is not right."

"And tell them what Ruby? You gone incriminate yourself? And me? We can never tell anyone about this. You do that and it won't end well. For either of us." Cuddy remarked, gently pulling Ruby into his arms for a kiss. She was obviously shaken by the implications of what could happen if she made the wrong decision. Ruby was confused and once again at Cuddy's mercy. The folks behind Christal's kidnapping were certainly dangerous and with far reaching abilities. Cuddy didn't believe that they could trust anyone at this point, the police included. Cuddy never saw cops around, but he was almost certain that cops were on their payroll. Ruby was reluctant to follow Cuddy to the back room.

His bedroom wall was filled with posters of San Francisco 49ers paraphernalia and his favorite wide receiver, Jerry Rice. His bed was perfectly made military style, a technique he learned serving a short bid in juvenile detention. Ruby shot a suspicious look at Cuddy over her shoulder when the door closed behind them. Cuddy says, "believe it or not, I do have a plan." He took Ruby by the hand. "I just need to know that you got my back."

"Wait, what are we doing in here. My girl is gone and I'm here with you." Ruby sighed in frustration. "I'm not ready fo-"

"Ready for... What, you don't trust me."

"I think I've proven that already."

"I gotta kill Big Diaz."

"No the hell you don't, Cuddy!" Ruby was shocked.

"Ruby... They took Christal, but the photos I saw were all of you. It's you they want Ruby. Are you hearing me?" The poor girl erupted in tears. Cuddy snatched the blanket from the perfectly made bed, revealing an arson of weaponry. Ruby reacted as if a rattle snake was in front of her. It startled her.

"But it ain't happening under my watch," Cuddy reassured.

Ruby gawked at the assault rifle as Cuddy lifted it and shelled one in the chamber. She'd never seen this side of Cuddy. What was becoming of her life, and why was she hanging on to every word Cuddy said? She had loved him ever since she was seven years old. Once he laid everything out for her, strangely, murdering Big Diaz didn't sound like a bad idea. Cuddy knew the whereabouts of every location, Big Diaz visited within the last month. Ruby didn't realize how much his new job affected him. Cuddy hated it, but realized that he was in too deep to get out. Plus, the organization wasn't one that he could simply leave whenever he saw fit. Cuddy would be the first to admit that he was no killer, but targeting his girl was an act that he couldn't afford to take lightly. Cuddy had to adapt to his current circumstances, which meant, that he had to be just as relentless as his adversary's. Cuddy preferred peace over war any day, but for Ruby, he'd crush a rock.

From the moment Cuddy stole a glance at Ruby's photos, he knew Big Diaz was living on borrowed time. First, Cuddy planned to rip Big Diaz off for every dime he had.

"I gotta do what I got to do, Ruby. You're afraid, I get it, but so am I. I'm gonna kill that mother fucker and thats all there is to it. If I don't, I got a bad feeling you'll be next."

"I need to get home, Cuddy."

"Okay, cool. I'll make arrangements to get you back home. But if you leave now, I don't know when the next time we may see each other." Ruby wanted to be with him badly. She was aware of the guns. Ruby saw the Teflon vest, and she'd heard him out, yet all she simply wanted was to be held and caressed by him. This was all too much for her young adolescent mind to comprehend.

"The word is probably out about Christal. Your mama gonna be looking for you babe."

"I don't care Cuddy." Ruby has a sudden change of heart. "I can't deal with this shit right now. Just kiss me will you."

CHAPTER 15

The empty seat in the classroom gave the room an awkward feeling. It was day three of Christal's abduction. The school was aware of her disappearance by now. Christal's absence caused a major distraction for everyone, the teachers and school counselors included. The principle approved teachers to assemble supporters together to hold a prayer vigil in the exact same place Katrina had hers. Local news covered their story with the question posed, *'were their abductions connected?'*

By now, investigators were aware of the girl's close connection. That they were best friends from as early as grade school. The police department were developing a profile in a gruelingly attempt to break the case. An abandon van that fit the description of the vehicle that drove Christal away, was found set ablaze just hours after the abduction. There was no evidence left at the scene, nor any signs of the aspiring track star anywhere.

The city's children were under attack. As if the genocidal warfare amongst the youth wasn't enough, this outrageous assault on the city's melanated girls, was enough to try the patience of a saint. The kidnappings were not isolated events. Perhaps the city had its own terrorist. A stalker or freak of some sort that specifically targeted brown girls. Tragically, authorities scratched their heads, clueless to their great city's treachery.

Ms. Battle held the vigil at school. None of this made sense to her. Katrina and Christal were two of her favorites. The most charismatic students to ever grace her classroom. This was so not right, another empty seat in her classroom. News about Christal absolutely devastated the teacher. The recent discussion with Ruby had a lot to do with her gloom. Ruby's words haunted her. The teenager practically predicted this nightmare. She thought of Ruby often. No one had heard a word from her. Aside from Christal's family, Ruby had to be taking this thing hard. Christal was her ace. Ruby's mom alerted the school early the next morning after the incident. Supposedly, Ruby was under the weather and would be out of school for a while. Ms. Battle found Linda's excuse quite odd giving the circumstances. She did not believe for one second that Ruby was sick. Its like Ruby said. *'Katrina last year. It could be me this year.'* Ruby's dreadful forewarning tormented her.

Would Ruby be the next girl to be taken? And leave Ms. Battle with three empty desks. The teacher's fable heart couldn't take anymore. Why wasn't there more of an outrage for our girls? Ms. Battle's gut was stewing up something more sinister. And the very thought terrified her. She found herself standing outside Ruby's front door after school at 5:30 pm. Ms. Battle thought long and hard about imposing on the family. But for the sake of her piece of mind, she needed to make sure Ruby was okay.

CHAPTER 16

Ruby didn't expect visitors. But to look out of the window and find mom and Ms. Battle talking on the front porch made her smile. It seemed like ages since she left the house. Her little stunt with Cuddy the other night, earned her a first-class seat in solitary confinement. It seemed that way at times. Ruby had pushed her mom too far. After Christal's appearance, Ruby had the nerve to not call home. And on top of that, she was out way past her curfew. Linda was pissed at her daughter for being so irresponsible, and nearly put hands on Ruby that night. She was punished and severely lectured for her actions. And then naturally as any loving parents would do, Ruby was showered with love. Despite Ruby's immature behavior, it was only by God's grace that their girl was back home with her family. Its a pain that Christal wasn't so lucky.

Linda was not having it with Ruby. She was all over her from this point on. Linda vowed that if some low life son of a bitch comes to try and steal her daughter away, it would most certainly be over her dead body. Linda suspected Ruby wasn't being completely honest. She couldn't quite put her finger on it, but Ruby was different. It was as if her little girl had morphed into a young lady right before her eyes. Already, she was excellent at keeping secrets. Linda wondered did her daughter know more than what she was letting on. Even the news reports hinted at a possible connection between Katrina and Christal's abductions.

Linda personally knew these girls. She helped plan their birthday parties. And now to speak to their mothers over the phone, or run into them in the streets, she got to witness their misery firsthand. It's an experience, Linda never wanted to live. If her daughter's closest friends were abducted a year a part, there's no reason to think, Ruby was an exception. It literally tore Linda apart to know a predator out there would take her daughter away from her. Linda cried herself to sleep every night since she'd learned of this shady abduction business.

Mom and Ms. Battle end their talk after nearly thirty minutes of chatting. As the teacher is walking away, she cast a quick glance up at the bedroom window and find Ruby there. Ms. Battle froze in her tracks, and student and teacher shared a moment. It was odd. Ruby looked aged and scared. Ruby moved away from the window when her mother turned to see what caught the teachers attention. Linda snickered inside at the curtain's movement,

Cuddy warned her to not leave the house. To not trust anyone. If she told her mom, Linda would call the police immediately. And Cuddy feared the police's loyalty was one sided. Wherever Ruby went, she was reminded of Christal.

The unwanted attention made her feel uncomfortable. Cuddy said it all would be over soon. Was she a fool to put so much faith in one person? She hadn't said a word to her mother about what she knew, and she didn't feel good about it. Seeing Katrina and Christal's face on the news last night was surreal. As a result, it put the spotlight on Ruby. People gawked at her in public, hugging her like they'd never see her again. She absolutely hated it.

The door opens and its Linda standing with her arms folded across her chest. Ruby is on the floor by the bedroom window, but jumps up startled at her mom's surprise entrance. "Hi ma, what's up with Ms. Battle?"

"Worried about you like everyone else." Linda says, taking a step inside Ruby's room. "She was just checking in on you." Linda exhales a sigh. "Wash the dishes for me, so I can cook dinner." On her way out, Linda stopped in the doorway. With accusing eyes, Linda's countenance dropped as she turned and faced her daughter. "Ruby, when were you gonna tell me about the knife you took to school? I see you've been busy." Ruby is tongue-tied and unable to offer a reply. Linda sees her struggling and smile. "Don't worry, I get it. Your teacher said you two talked. I... I just wish you could trust me more. If you are afraid.... I'm your mama, why not talk to me?" With that said, Linda left the room. She didn't wait on a response from Ruby. Over her shoulder, she yelled, "don't forget the dishes."

__Ms. Battle snitch me out!__ Ruby said to no one in particular.

CHAPTER 17

Cuddy didn't know what to expect when he met with Big Diaz today. He knew they didn't trust him. And that being anywhere near Big Diaz's operation was a serious risk for him. The people he worked for were picking off his childhood friends like cherries off a cherry tree. Even worse, they foolishly expected Cuddy to turn a cowardly blind eye. Cuddy suspected that he was expendable to the top branch. Perhaps there were lengthy discussions on what to do with him. Not long after his arrival, Cuddy was summoned to a spacious room inside the night club where Big Diaz, Kenny and Mark waited for him. He thought it was odd that ,Tina was the only bartender present, but left shortly after letting him in. Tina's suspect behavior put him on high alert.

With the door closing behind him, Cuddy knew his chances of making it out alive were slim. He was instantly drilled about missing photos. Cuddy allowed them to speak without interrupting. And when they were done, he didn't deny their claims. In fact, he did something totally unexpected. Cuddy admitted to taking the photos. He said he took them to hold as evidence.

"The photos are in a safe place. If you don't touch my girl. I will never speak a word of this to anyone."

"You're right about one thing, that's for sure," Kenny interjects, turning to Big Diaz for conformation. "You're never talking to no one ever again." Cuddy doesn't budge. He was warned not to come, and to leave well enough alone. Allow the authorities to take over before anyone else got hurt. Big Diaz finally take a step forward with this awful God forsaking smirk on his face.

"You should be worried young, Cuddy. Depending on who my friend is today, you just may be fucked!" Big Diaz cast a quick glance over at Mark.

"You not gunman today, is you Camera-, I mean Mark." Big Diaz cackles. Kenny grins. Cuddy appears dumbfounded to what looked to be an inside joke between them. But then he saw something glisten at the tip of Mark's fingertips. Initially, Cuddy doesn't think much of it. Mark is calm, collective and observant to everyone present. He looked across at Cuddy with contempt in his eyes, then he turned to Big Diaz saying, "I warned you about him. You've fucked us." Marks says finally. "I'm blade man today by the way." Mark barely finishes his statement before the jagged edge knife swings maliciously at Big Diaz's throat. The movement is so swift and affective, that the giant falls instantly to the floor, gasping for breath with his massive hands wrapped around his leaking throat.

No one expected such a ruthless act from Mark. Cuddy perhaps. He sensed an ill vibe, he just didn't know what it was. Kenny drew his weapon with firm precision. But by this time, Mark had miraculously replaced his blade with a fire spitting nine milli meter. Hot shells exchanged in a hail of gun fire. Both men heartlessly drill one another down, leaving one hell of a stench of gun powder and gun smoke.

Cuddy slowly came alive, peeking an eye over the counter top where he momentarily took shelter when the bullets started flying. Bodies are twitching with desolate sounds of life. Cuddy cautiously tiptoed over splatters of blood, stopping at movement from Mark. His finger twitched, he farted and stunk up the place. With three wounds to his chest, the bastard courageously clung to life. Cuddy had had all that he could take. He took the 38 Special concealed in his back and put Mark out of his misery with one shot to his face. Cuddy nearly vomited from the blow back.

Cuddy's adrenaline is through the ruff now. He moved fast once he was sure that everyone was down and there was no sign of life. He raced to the control room and swiftly ejected the surveillance tape. Then he dashed to another room that contained a huge safe that happened to be cracked, but void of any substance.

Panic sets in momentarily for Cuddy, but then his brain is smacked with a burst of relief. He ran out of the room and over to the bar counter top. Hidden underneath the bar beside a medium size safe, are two huge duffel bags filled with cash. From his back pocket, he retrieved a ski mask and pulled it over his face. He was now in this thing deep, and there was no turning back. He absolutely could not get caught here. He hoped to make a clean get away and avoid having to hurt anyone else. Cuddy was amped. He tried to breathe through his nose as he moved hastily.

"I'm coming out heavy my nigga, stand by." Cuddy spat into a handheld device he kept off and secured inside his jacket pocket. Cuddy lodged the duffel bags over both shoulders and charged toward the entrance. Lil Jay is there waiting outside in a stolen, dark blue Ford Eddie Bauer XLT. Cuddy tossed him one of the duffel bags and dashed around to the other side. He threw his bag in the rear, and then he jumped in the passenger seat.

"Stomp this bitch nigga! To the spot to dump the cash and don't stop this motherfucker for nobody!" Lil Jay veered to the right to jump on the interstate while Cuddy pulled his jacket off and snatched off his Teflon vest underneath. As far as Cuddy was concerned, the riddled men back at the night club were simply garbage that needed to be taken out. The world would be much better off without them. The massacre wouldn't go unnoticed, and the stolen cash would draw in blood hounds. For Cuddy, the plan could not have gone any smoother. If the results left Big Diaz dead and Cuddy with bags of cash, then the risk was well worth the reward.

48

CHAPTER 18

The murder scene was atrocious in a community not accustomed to this level of violence. Folks heard the deafening shots, but no witnesses had come forth at this time. Det. Destiny was on the scene along with a slew of law enforcement, leaving no stone unturned in getting to the bottom of what happen. The victims were in the largest room in the building. A spacey lounge area that could be used for anything from conducting business meetings, to hosting event parties. Crime scene investigators are first on the scene. Police officers arrive and immediately secure the crime scene. They photograph the victims, collect evidence and mark shell casings. There are three fatalities. Det. Destiny discovers a breakthrough while the crime scene investigators are snapping photos.

He stands over one of the deceased victims. The guy clutching a nasty neck wound, was a clear indication that John Doe's throat had been slit savagely. Now this struck the detective as odd. In ten years of working homicides, thugs only busted guns, not slit throats. To get a better understanding of what occurred, crime scene investigators took measurements of the crime scene, and relative locations of evidence and bodies. No victims had been identified, so for clarity, they went by John Doe one, two and three. Det. Destiny moved over to John Doe two.

The detective swiftly located the murder weapon that took out John Doe one. John Doe two had at least three wounds to his chest and one to his face. A crime scene investigator carefully lifted the blood-stained, blade case attached to the victims pants belt, and secured it carefully into a plastic Ziploc bag. The detective concluded that perhaps the killings were the result of a botched shootout. While investigators examined and preserved the evidence for the lab, the detective took a tour of the crime scene. He walked outside, hoping to locate witnesses. They knocked on neighboring doors. The detective gathered from speaking to home owners, that many of them weren't too fond of the night club. There sure wasn't a welcoming comity for the party goers. Neighbors complained about everything from loud music, to half naked girls, wandering around at weird hours of the morning.

At least two hours pass before the detective began to wrap up his crime scene. He's on his way to the station when he's approached by a fellow officer with a southern accent. "Detective, this young lady says she works here." The timid lady was about 5'2 in height, and brown skin with a slim physique. She was edgy as she stepped forward, wearing a fitting white t-shirt with pink and blue letters that read, Tina, (Bartender). The frighten woman had been working earlier in the day, but was discharged early. The detective took Tina to the first conference room on the left to avoid the crime scene. The bartender was shown photos of the deceased and was able to identify them all. Tina became deafly silent when asked if anyone else besides the deceased were there upon her leaving. "Someone else was here. Tell me." The detective pressed. She shrugged her shoulders and shifted nervously in her seat. "This could be an important break in the case. If someone was here, it could mean they possibly witness what happen."

"I don't know about all that. Cuddy's a cool kid."

"Cuddy? That's his name?"

"That's what everyone called him."

Prior to Cuddy's arrival, Tina overheard Big Diaz tell Kenny that Cuddy had to go. Big Diaz was against it, but said the request had come down from on high. Big Diaz said Cuddy had done something terribly stupid. And that he couldn't save him. She was told to take off early afterwards. She was shook up bad when Cuddy appeared like Michael Myers at the front door. She cringed at the mere thought of their run-in long after she left. To hear what she heard, and see the man right before he was to walk into his own slaughter was horrifying. And to come back to work hours later and find out the total opposite occurred. This made no sense to her.

Tina was afraid. She thought that she should tell someone about what she overheard, but she didn't want to be involved. She wasn't particularly comfortable with talking to the police, but they could possibly be useful to her down the line. The detective wouldn't allow Tina to catch another Taxi back home. He gave her a lift on his way back to the station. The detective arrived at Tina's place within a matter of minutes. She turned to the detective before opening the door. "Do you think I'm safe?" Tina was a nervous wreck. She couldn't stop looking around. Then the detective snaps her back.

"Is there a reason why you think you're not safe, Tina?"

"Just forget about it." Tina opened her door.

"No wait," the detective says, reaching for her arm. He sighed and with a hint of compassion in his voice, he says, "if it's any consolation, there is no reason why anyone should want to harm you. You saw this guy on your way out, big deal. Relax, get some rest. You were a big help. Call me morning, noon or night."

There was a hint of hope in Tina's eyes. "Okay, I hope you're right." Stepping out of the car, her eyes darted in every which direction before she cautiously dashed up to her apartment.

At-Tariq The Comer by Night

CHAPTER 19

Meanwhile, parked inconspicuously on the same street at least two vehicles down from Tina's place, faceless men sat virtually unnoticed in a Dodge minivan with covered license plates. The bearded man in the passenger seat adjusted his binoculars to a second vehicle and zoomed in on its target.

"He handed her a card."

"If she's working with the police, this could be too risky to pursue," the driver says worried.

"It could be at least a half a million on this take. The risk is worth the reward," the passenger replies never losing focus. He stared through the binoculars like a hungry lion after a meal. Losing Big Diaz and his hooligans was a major blow for the organization. Big Diaz was a money horse and covered a lot of ground in not just the city, but all of Central Virginia. And losing him meant a major decrease in funds for everyone involved.

A swift and severe message needed to be sent to the responsible parties. Many of the foot soldiers felt that way. However, the higher-ups and decision makers didn't share the same sentiment. They were entrenched in a billion-dollar industry that showed no signs of its services ever being out of demand. Big Diaz was important to their recruitment process. Young vulnerable girls flocked to Big Diaz like bees on honey. He gave them hope, made false promises to win their trust before rocking their worlds. The girls awakened in foreign places, drugged and confused out of their minds. Big Diaz had a bag for the bosses. But now he was gone, leaving their entire operation at risk and no idea where to locate their cash. This infuriated them. "Who has the money, the cops or this snot nose son of a bitch?"

Down the street

"Did this bitch just get out an unmarked police car?" Lil Jay utters in pure disbelief. The black Suburban hadn't too long drove up. It had been sitting there with the lights out a short while before the unmarked vehicle arrived. Lil Jay turned to Cuddy in the passenger seat who appeared to be visually annoyed by Tina's actions. In trying to process everything that he'd witness back at Big Diaz's night club, Cuddy unsuccessfully tried to eliminate any potential threat that could haunt him later. The bartender made the top pick. She was the only living witness who could put him at the murder scene. Cuddy only wished he could've thought of it sooner. He tried to imagine how it all may have looked to her. He felt compelled to contact her immediately. He spoke to Tina that day as he walked in, and he recall her not returning the gesture. Her energy was way off for sure. Now Cuddy understood why.

"I didn't say anything back at Tina's spot, but I peeped a van parked out there. Shit looked suspect."

"Now you tell me? So nigga, and?"

"Don't look back now, but the same van is behind us, Cuddy. I peeped it then but was unsure. No tags, I'm almost sure we're being followed. Why the fuck would someone be following us?" Lil Jay said nervously.

"I got a half a million reasons why," answers Cuddy.

CHAPTER 20

Ruby didn't know what to do. She'd been calling Cuddy ever since she heard the news of Big Diaz. The neighborhood was shocked to find out about his unfortunate demise. Where was Cuddy and why hadn't he reached out to her? She hated this, the waiting and the worrying. Ruby finally got the nerve to sit her mom down after the news of Big Diaz. She leveled with Linda about what really went down, but kept out the part of Cuddy killing Big Diaz. Linda was absolutely devastated, and couldn't believe how caught up Ruby was in all this.

Linda called Ruby's dad and brought him up to speed on Ruby's drama. Naturally, dad was shocked and angry to learn what his daughter had been up to. Her parents bit a chunk out of her. They really let her have it for being so reckless. For keeping a secret that affected the lives of so many. Despite it all, Ruby felt relieved to finally share her burden. She was drained, and needed her parents to step in and take control of the wheel before she crashed.

Linda thought it was time to involve the police. Although Ruby was afraid, she reluctantly agreed to allow the professionals to take over. She felt horrible enough inside for not calling sooner. Perhaps Christal would still be here. But she didn't want to talk to the police until she consulted with Cuddy. Unfortunately, that request would never happen. She spotted the detective drive up from her bedroom window. A suited dark man with a distinctive beard. The car he got out of appeared to be an unmarked police car. From the way guys in the neighborhood reacted to his presence, Ruby was certain he was a cop. In the past, Ruby never understood the uneasiness folks got from run-ins with the police until today. She felt every ounce of that anxiety when the detective turned toward her apartment. She freaked out.

The neighborhood was just the way the detective remembered when he was just a city cop working his way up through the ranks. The dealers were the same, only their faces had changed over the years. He knew that his mere presence there invoked uneasiness and put everyone on high alert. The men scrambled around to put as much distance between them and the detective as humanely possible. But he wasn't there to give them a hard time. Not today at least. Something more sinister brought Det. Destiny to Ruby's doorstep. He knocked at the front door, waited and in seconds, he was let in by a middle aged attractive ebony skinned lady. As she was closing the door, Linda made a mental note of her neighbor's reckless eye bawling her as she pushed the door shut. She would certainly have some explaining to do.

Ruby had been prolonging from coming downstairs for at least ten minutes while Linda and the detective waited. She paced her bedroom quarters in a frantic desperation. She was not prepared to talk to the police. Not without Cuddy. Where the hell was Cuddy? Big Diaz had been dead for two days now and she couldn't think of one single reason why Cuddy hadn't called her. Ruby was beginning to worry. If he survived, why wouldn't he contact her? Did he get locked up? Perhaps the detective's presence here could render the answers that she so craved.

"Okay Ruby, you got this girl," she began saying for encouragement. She eventually got herself together and made her way downstairs.

Upon entering the living room where her mom and the detective were sitting, the first thing she noticed was a manila envelope on the oakwood table. Linda bit down on her bottom lip when she was nervous, a habit Ruby's dad often teased her about. Ruby saw her mom chewing down on her bottom lip and was shook to the core. Ruby was assured by the detective that she was in no trouble. He mentioned his murder case, and showed them mug shots of Big Diaz. The detective observed Ruby's reaction. Linda watched the detective. She wasn't particularly fond of the police sitting in her living room. Ruby's dad was working at Dupont, and wouldn't be able to get off in time. The detective thought Ruby's input could be vital to their investigation. Ruby identified Big Diaz, said she knew him from the neighborhood, but never had any dealings with him.

"Are you absolutely sure about that?" She hesitated her next statement, turning to her mother for support.

"Think hard, Ruby," mom encouraged. That's when it hit her. The day at the track meet. She told the detective about it.

"And your friend, Christal was there, correct?" Ruby nodded solemnly.

"What if I told you, Christal and Katrina's abductions could possibly be connected." The room became deafly silent.

"Oh my God," came Linda's reply. She's wiping away tears. Ruby on the other hand, the detective can't read. What did she know?

"These were your friends, Ruby."

The detective pushed the manila envelope toward Ruby for her inspection. She did nothing for a brief moment, but stare at the thing as if it were some unknown wonder. The detective observed her closely. "Ruby, honey." Linda eyes her daughter with suspicion.

"Oh, sorry," Ruby says finally breaking her trance. He couldn't put a finger on it, but something about Ruby's behavior was unsettling. She pulled photos from the envelope and began leafing through them. Her heart fluttered and she shook like a leaf on a windy day. The pictures were of her, Katrina and Christal. Linda was shaken. "Detective, what the hell is going on? Why are there pictures of my daughter?"

"Maybe Ruby can tell us." Ruby doesn't utter one word. The trio were just little girls goofing around at the park. Christal got off the merry-go-round so that Ruby could get her turn. Ruby jumped on. Katrina and Christal secretly in on an inside joke, began pushing Ruby fiercely, *around and round, around and round.* The girls finally stopped their cruel joke. Ruby stumbled off the merry-go-round woozy, and barely able to walk, feeling like she'd puke at any second. Ironically, it's how she felt at the present with this bastard detective breathing down her neck. Her head spun like she'd just stumbled off that darn merry-go-round.

"I'm just gonna state the obvious here," The detective says with a hint of frustration in his tone, never taking his focus away from Ruby. "We have evidence that links Cuddy to the triple homicide. At the same crime scene, we found this evidence of you and your friends. Two of which has been abducted. You are the only one left, Ruby." When the detective is done, he says to Ruby, "but you already know that right?"

"Whats this supposed to mean detective," mom commanded to know.

"Just..." The detective sighs, turning to Linda with concern. His eyes never left Ruby. "I think Ruby knows more than she's letting on. She didn't seem surprised at all to see these photos. Almost as if she'd seen them before."

"What is Cuddy doing? What's his involvement in all this? His life could be in danger. It would do you some good to cooperate with us fully." The detective waited on her reaction. Evidently, Cuddy meant a great deal to her to make her eyes light up at the mention of his name. And from the looks of it, the detective hit a nerve.

"Where is he Ruby?"

Ruby tried to read him. Obviously, he had pieces of the truth, but just how much did this cop know? Ruby didn't speak. She didn't know what to say. Cuddy was supposed to guide her through this most important part. Boy did he manage to drop the ball this time. Just when her mom is about to jump down her throat for being a mute, the house phone suddenly rings on the kitchen wall. Linda jumps out of her socks with fear. Finally, Ruby's dad was returning her call. The last thing she wanted was to face this alone. She dashed to the kitchen, retrieving the phone. In seconds, comes "wait a minute, Cuddy?" Linda tries to whisper into the receiver. She nervously turned her back to the living room for no apparent reason. Ruby and the detective are up out of their seats at the same time upon hearing, Cuddy's name. "Well... Cu Cuddy..." Linda never stuttered. "Ruby is busy right now... Excuse me?" Linda looked pass Ruby, and confusingly at the detective with the phone held out.

"Just a moment, Ruby. I, well he wants to speak to the detective..." Cuddy's call freaks everyone in the room out, the detective included. He looked alarmed. Was Cuddy sitting outside their place casing the joint? Ruby flew to the window for a peek. She didn't see anything out of the ordinary. How was this so? Countless hours of waiting on his call, Ruby thought Cuddy had forgotten her. Backed into a corner by the detective and his aggressive questioning, Ruby wanted to tear her hair out and scream from the pressure. All she knew was from the moment he arrived, she had been praying for divine intervention.

She wanted her life back. She wanted her friends back. Ruby would give anything to fuss with Christal right now. And Katrina with her conceited self, she missed the fieriest competitions between them. Their hilarious arguments over boys, and the girls all trying to outdo one another. The pain and void she felt in her heart from missing them, was an ache that would remain there until her girls returned. She needed this to end. And the unexpected call from Cuddy, she hoped would be an answer to her prayers. ***But just what the hell was Cuddy up to?***

Det. Destiny reluctantly accepted the phone, placing it to his ear. Ruby cringed inside at the way the detective examined her. What could Det. Destiny be thinking?

CHAPTER 21

Back at the police station, the interrogation room was deafly silent, and buttered popcorn was the only thing missing. Cuddy arrived in a room full of piranhas. Big Diaz, Kenny and Mark were present. There was a brief exchange between them, and hell unleashed. Big Diaz was slaughtered mercilessly,and one thing lead to another. Bullets reigned supreme, tearing through flesh, ricocheting through walls, shattering windows and terrifying neighboring residents. When the smoke cleared, Cuddy was the only man standing. He peaked his head over the counter top, and slowly stood to his feet, terror stuck. The strangest thing happened. The tape stopped and the screen conveniently went blank. Law enforcement stood around with their mouths hung open for the next act. But nothing came, which the detective found interesting.

Cuddy sat seemingly unbothered behind the one-way glass where a gang of law enforcement observed him closely from the other side. Cuddy had done a good deed for the department. He surrendered himself willingly, connected dots to their case that otherwise would have taken them weeks to uncover. Cuddy confirmed Tina's account of them running into one another on her way out of the night club. Cuddy explained to the detective that he was simply a victim of circumstance. He didn't want to hang in the streets or steal cars like the rest of his peers. And so, he ran across Big Diaz one day in the neighborhood, and asked him if he could set him up with a legitimate gig.

Cuddy chose what he felt were the lesser of two evils. Cuddy came prepared to level with the detective about his involvement.

"Look detective, I want to put an end to whoever is behind this just as much as you. They took two of my friends. And I'm afraid that, Ruby could be next. They kept me out of the business, and the only reason I didn't leave the minute I found out, is because of the photos I found of Ruby. I figured I could help her more if I was on the inside.

"And tell me, why is Ruby so important to them? With all this heat, why would they even risk going back to get her?"

"Because she's rare. Untouched if you know what I mean."

"You mean, Ruby is a virgin?"

"That's right, she's pure as a dove." Cuddy states with a hint of pride.

"What else are you not telling me Mr. Sampson?"

"I don't know what you mean detective."

"The money Mr. Sampson?." The detective sighs before looking across at Cuddy. "We know about the large amount of cash at the club that night."

"I have no clue what you mean. Detective, you only saw the tape, but I was there. And I wasn't about to waste time looking for anything. I got out the first chance I got."

"Speaking of the tape, Mr. Sampson. Why cut it? What are you hiding?"

"Boom!" Cuddy flinches as he's smacked with a burst of unwanted images from the night in question. It was as if the detective had struck a nerve. The brazing shootout and blow back from torn flesh as men went a tumbling down before him like dominoes. Cuddy saw himself commit his first murder. He felt convicted with each word the detective spoke.

"What did you do after the shooting? I get it. What's revealed in the tape clears you of murder. But the witness places you at the scene of the crime along with everyone who died. The witness claims to have assisted in counting a very large sum of money."

"Boom!!" A pair of legs is tossed in the trunk. Lil Jay shuts the trunk and looks across at Cuddy. "Don't feel sorry for this bitch, she shouldn't be running her fucking mouth." Lil Jay slammed the trunk shut. Cuddy finally lifted his head and gazed across at the detective. "Your witness detective, are you sure she's reliable?"

"You're not completely innocent Sampson. You worked for these people. You left a crime scene. You could be charged with accessory after the fact. Not to mention tampering with a homicide investigation. Do you see where I'm going with this? I can't think of one reason why you would take that surveillance tape, other than the fact that it incriminates you. And if that is the case, it makes perfect sense why you would take it. You erased whatever you needed to. It makes me wonder what else you took from the club."

"Pure speculation detective. You would have to prove all of that. In good faith, I brought you the tape. I never said I took it from the club. I'm surprised, Tina didn't already tell you yet."

"Tell me what?" Det. Destiny eyed Cuddy with suspicion.

"That she gave it to me. How else would I have gotten it, she's the employee."

"Really, is that right?" Det. Destiny was now visibly annoyed. Cuddy didn't budge or bat an eye. The interrogation door opened suddenly, and the detective was summoned by a chubby, reddish cheek police officer.

"No word on our witness," the officer remarked the moment he had Det. Destiny's attention. "What are you thinking detective?"

"That this son of bitch, Sampson is a wise ass. Funny how he says that he got the tape from our witness. Its bullshit, no way she gave him that tape."

"Speaking of her, it's the second time we sent a unit to check on her. Nobody's heard a word, not even her mother."

'*You would have to prove all of that.*' "That's what he said to me," "Okay, so?"

"He knows I can't prove it." The detective glares intently through the glass at Cuddy who seems to be momentarily occupied with tossing up candy, and catching it with his mouth. Cuddy's lack of concern made the detective's blood boil. What did this bastard know?

"You think the witness could be missing?"

"I'm not completely sure... but we may never find her... Alive. I should have protected her."

"Our witness?" The officer asked still confused. He was struggling to wrap his mind around what happened.

"I pray that I'm wrong," Det. Destiny comments regrettably.

"What do we do with this ass hole in the meantime, detective?"

"We can't hold him. Let him go. But his ass is dirty, one way or the other, I'm taking him down. He's not riding off into the sunset. Put a tail on him for now. Send another unit to Tina's place. Her mom may want to file a missing person's report.

CHAPTER 22

The front page of the Times Weekly read, *"64,000 Missing Black Girls in the United States and NO ONE Seems to Care."* The count for missing girls were steadily increasing. Congregated prayer vigils were the new norm. A different adduction meant a different family mourning. The neighborhood where Ruby lived had immense police presence due to the recent crimes. Now that the word was out, residents were aware that evil folk in their own neighborhood could possibly be co-conspirators.

The boys in blue were leaving no stones unturned. They walked the streets, chatted with dealers, and knocked on doors to try and establish a line of communication with the residents who lived there. And they got mixed emotions at times. The people were reluctant and afraid of law enforcement for many reasons, some of which were legitimate. But with this new problem, many of the residents cooperated with the police. Law enforcement were virtually clueless without the help of the people on the ground. This shady abduction business was a harsh assault on the city and its residents.

Tanisha Anderson, known by her peers as *Tina the bartender*, was the latest victim to disappear without so much as a trace. No one had seen or heard a word from Tina in weeks. Law enforcement advised the public that the investigation was ongoing. Before releasing Cuddy back to the streets, the detective warned him that his life could be in danger. Supporters of Big Diaz wanted retribution for Big Diaz's demise. His family members were skeptical of the police's account. No one who personally knew the guys believed for one second, that they offed one another in such a brutal way. There was even a rumor that it was the police behind the killings. Folks in the neighborhood were far reaching, believing that perhaps the victims were a part of a secret cult that took them out.

The police were not screwing around with Cuddy, they wanted his full cooperation. The veteran detective threatened to bring the full weight of the police department down on his head if not. They would probably link him to the murders and maliciously snitch him out to Big Diaz's people if he didn't comply. That alone would certainly get Cuddy hit.

They had him in their cross hairs and Cuddy knew it. Law enforcement wanted to stash the pair away in protective custody. They feared with Tina missing, Ruby and Cuddy could be next. The authorities put tails on them both. School was unpleasant. The police escorts to and from school turned Ruby into a nervous wreck. From here on out, this would be her new norm. It was prison minus the bars, and Linda was the bully warden. Ruby's mom wouldn't let up. Because of her tight grip, Ruby hardly saw Cuddy at all.

She was warned to not go near him. Apparently, he was the reason behind her chaos. Never mind him being the exact reason she hadn't been abducted. They were totally oblivious to what was truly going on. What had become of her life? Tournaments were right around the corner, but how could she compete at a time like this? Chrystal was not here, how dare anyone to expect her to give a shit about anything right now. Things had changed. She cared less. Ruby did nothing wrong, yet she was being penalized for something that was clearly not her fault.

CHAPTER 23

Dennis pulled out his jimmy as he approached a brand-new Jeep inside the parking garage of a luxurious Hilton Inn. A few swift movements and Dennis had the driver's door unlocked. With his screw driver, he hurriedly popped the ignition switch, connected a few wires and within seconds, the truck's engine roared. Terrance dressed in identical attire as Cuddy, climbed into the front seat with Lil Jay. As the silver Expedition drove off fast, Cuddy jumped inside the jeep with Dennis. It took three cars for Cuddy to shake his captures. He had at least two tails on him that he was aware of. Boy what a relief to finally be out from under the watchful eye of law enforcement. They took the bait. They always did. He was exhausted with this dog and pony race.

The cops wanted him. Big Diaz's murder left many unanswered questions. He had over a half million of his employer's blood money that never made the drop. The money didn't get buried with him, that they were certain of. Cuddy was their only lead. They watched him around the clock. If they surveyed him long enough, perhaps he'd slip up. The gang's superb skills as car thieves, kept them a few steps ahead of their pursuers. They'd have cars reserved for Cuddy just to move him around the city.

He missed Ruby. The absence between them slowly ate away at his soul. He arrived at the high school just in time to spot, Ruby exiting the bus. He tried to get her attention, crossing the street disguised in a green and black Eagles hoodie. Cuddy took a drag off his Newport when a white unmarked Sedan, emerged through a haze of his cigarette smoke . The car slowly drove up and halted for a pair of school kids, crossing the street. Ruby is the fifth student off the bus. Just the mere sight of her was a breath of fresh air. Cuddy wanted to yell out her name and alert her to his presence. Regrettably, the act would only expose him. Her head swayed every which way as if she too was looking for someone. As if she felt his presence, Ruby casted a glance over her shoulder just in time to see Cuddy spin on his heels and toss his hood over his head. She noticed his walk, opened her mouth in an attempt to get his attention, but too much distance had gotten between them.

Her friends were bombarding her. School officials were ushering students into the building, but Ruby could only think of Cuddy. Out of nowhere, an unmarked car cruised slowly by her. The occupants turned their faces away to avoid eye contact with Ruby.

Back inside the car, Cuddy gave Lil Jay the thumbs down with a face wreaking disappointment. "I didn't get to see her." Cuddy says and sighs visibly upset. "She got a tail on her man. And I don't know if it's the police or worse." His face is fearful, afraid because there was no sure way to determine who was watching her. Then there were his thoughts. They were downright disturbing when reflecting on what he'd do to anyone who violated his girl. He didn't like where this dark road of despair was leading him. But there was no turning back now. Cuddy and his crew had killed before. If the need arose again, the boys wouldn't hesitate to cover their blood trail. He went through a lot this morning to be at Ruby's school. He just wished he could've talk to her today, even if just for one minute. Cuddy missed his girl.

CHAPTER 24

Ruby set goals for herself. She had planned assignments to accomplish during these important years of her life. Somehow, things had gone terribly wrong. With Christal's disappearance and Cuddy's uncertain future hanging in the balance, Ruby was in a state of disbelief. She didn't understand what was happening. Why was she expected to simply go on as if all was fine when her life was a total wreck? *'Stay focus Ruby, keep your grades up baby girl.'* Blah blah blah!

School had become more of a freak show than a place of learning. Harsh stares, rude whispering and stupid questions, was just some of the absurdity Ruby endured. "Heard anything about Christal?"

"No, have you?" She hated the unwanted attention and detested her incredible vulnerability. She had this insane paranoia, that perhaps she would be taken just like her friends. The unmarked police assigned to protect her didn't make her feel any safer. What if they were on the payroll? And why was Cuddy treated like the criminal? No calls, no visits, what did she do to deserve this prison?

It's the first day of the tournaments as Ruby prepare to takeoff. There's a moment where time stood still. She closed her eyes and took a deep breath. Christal was there glowing when she reopened them. Christal kneels to take her place. Katrina is on the opposite side of her. It was surreal. Her hair was braided superbly, six crisp braids to the back with an angelic presence. Screams from the sideline went unheard. Then Ruby heard the loud bang. Ruby took off late. She was momentarily lost in her thoughts. *'Why am I still competing?'* It finally hit her. The thrill and excitement was gone. Her childhood friends were still presumed missing. Without them, she just couldn't find the fun in it anymore. Anyone watching, Ruby could easily see that she wasn't completely there. And who could blame her for quitting the tournament, considering what she'd been through. She walked off the field.

It's finally the weekend and Ruby could relax and unwind. She told her mom that she needed air. That she would go nuts if she didn't get out of the house, and get some sense of normalcy back in her life. Linda was afraid for her daughter and felt Ruby was acting naive about it all.

"Mama, you can't keep me locked up in here like this. And why can't I see Cuddy?" Some of the girls from the neighborhood were getting together later at Hilltop Park. It used to be a thing she did with Katrina and Chrystal. That seemed like ages ago. Ruby was only allowed to hang out with her younger cousin, Yolanda. Ruby was on edge. She couldn't sleep. She couldn't keep still or eat. ***She was Cuddy sick***. Ruby and her cousin were finally allowed to walk to the store after pressing protest from Ruby. She was tired of everyone worrying about her and treating her like a baby.

Every year towards the end of the summer, the neighborhood residents got together and planned a marvelous barbeque for their cubs. Meanwhile, the kids would head down to the park to pass time while the food cooked. Ruby and her cousin, Yolanda were among the pack. The adults warned the adolescents to stay close together and to keep away from strangers. Linda knew that Ruby needed a break. Their home was full of tension, walking on eggshells in a pitiful attempt to avoid each other. Linda invited her sister over and they drank while preparing food for the cookout. She felt that allowing Ruby to go out and hang with her friends for a short while, could perhaps in some way help repair their broken relationship.

She had been extremely hard on Ruby and as a result, her daughter had completely shut down. Linda had been warned by members of the family to be careful. That her actions could push Ruby completely over the edge. Today, she turned over a new leaf. Linda drank more wine and laughed while her sister, Lucy danced to old school jams. The neighborhood was jumping with new life. Several grills were burning, Linda hadn't felt this good in a long time.

CHAPTER 25

City Park

There was a delightful laugh from an adorable ebony girl as she pounced upward into the air. The chubby kid on the other end of the seesaw with the crooked smile, pushed just a little too hard, causing the girl to fall off the seesaw and cry. Her mom mumbled something unfriendly at the overly aggressive boy while she tended to her daughter. A boy about five years of age with a bared chest, climbed the monkey bars like a jungle bred chimpanzee. He was amazingly gifted.

Teenagers made their way toward the rec center to hang out by the bathroom stall. A lot went on in that blind spotted area. Its where little girls morphed into hot teens, and boys flexed their manhood and exercised their best thinking from below the waist. A cute European couple are seated on the bench, overlooking the city's vast landscape. This is the time of rebellion. The great wall of silence, where adults aren't allowed. The adolescents smoked weed, popped pills and engaged in all kinds of silly young stuff to pass time and escape life's wild escapades.

Smoke haze filled the air. And every so often, a police cruiser would ride by. The dust hadn't settled on the recent kidnappings. The authorities kept a close watch, especially when there was a crowd of girls. This got the police's attention. In their minds, perhaps a group of girls would get the kidnappers attention. Thinking like a criminal could possibly warrant quick results.

Ruby Parker and cousin, Yolanda goes to the steps that lead down to Main street. There were less people around. Yalonda was her protege and wanted to compete as Ruby had once done. Ruby told her cousin that one significant reason for running for her, was that it gave her a sense of freedom. Instead of indulging in teenage rebellion, Ruby decided to work out and run step drills with her cousin. There was at least 40 yards of narrow stairs below them.

Yolanda was about to learn just what that track life be like today. For some time now, Yolanda had been pressuring Ruby to teach her. They took about ten minutes or so to warm up. They walked and stretched while

Ruby explained the benefits of stair climbing. Ruby started first down the narrow steps at a steady pace. She had perfect form and superb feet movement. Yalonda observed every detail. Ruby was swift, appearing to have more energy on the way back up. Ruby pushed it. Yalonda was amazed and super hyped as Ruby tagged her in. They had four sets to complete. Yalonda had done a great job up until the third set. She complained about her legs cramping up on her. Ruby quickly assisted, helped her finish her set, and then she flew down for her last climb. Yolanda was shocked. Ruby ran the last set like the first one. She was fantastic. Cheering her big cousin on, Yalonda suddenly noticed a blue minivan parked at the bottom of the steps where it hadn't been moments earlier.

Ruby didn't appear to notice it there as she turned on her heels to come back up the steps. Horrifyingly so, the rear door burst open and out jumps a masked figure. "OH MY GOD," Yolanda utters the words in pure disbelief.

"RUBY! Behind you!" Yalonda's screams are earth shattering. Her next move proved to be disastrous. Yolanda didn't know why she'd done it, but she lunged forward as the words left her mouth. She felt her tender hamstring snap, the pain nearly took her off her feet.

The abductor was all over Ruby as she attempted to react to her cousins near fatal warning. She's instantly snatched from behind, blind folded and thrown inside the van like a heap of garbage. The door slammed shut and the van burned rubber. Everyone in near distance stopped what they were doing to focus on Yolanda's terrifying expression as she lay there on the grass, clutching her left hamstring. She stared frantically into the distance with a face filled with horror.

"They took her! A man just took Ruby," the heart broken girl cried out to all who approached her. She pointed. "The blue van! You see it, you see it?" They gather around and focus their gaze down the hill and over the city's main street, and all of the downtown structure. But the van was long gone. And nothing seemed out of the ordinary. However, there was one thing everyone could agree on. Ruby was gone.

CHAPTER 26

Linda

Yolanda went over every detail of Ruby's abduction so many times, that the last interview brought her to tears. She was guilt stricken for the amount of pressure she put on Ruby to hangout with her. And now Ruby was gone because of it. But Linda wouldn't hear of her niece carrying on such a heavy burden.

"If it's anybody's fault, the blame lies here… with me." Linda states with strong conviction. Her sister offers a soothing hug as Linda agitatedly chews her bottom lip.

"I should never have allowed her to go to that park in the first place." Linda burst into tears.

Crime Scene

Det. Destiny is frozen outside the crime scene perimeter where Ruby had been taken. He searched for physical evidence. With only two escape routs, he predicted the interstate being their best choice. Heavy emotion filled his chest while positioned in the same location the escaped vehicle was parked. He feared the results if Ruby wasn't located in time. Protective custody would have prevented this, if only they'd listened. Walking off with the chief who stopped him for a word, an object glistened from the ground near his right foot. It was an oval shaped diamond necklace with a gold charm. He examined it while his chief went on about the case ahead. Det. Destiny was too occupied in his thoughts to answer. The detective had a good idea where the necklace had come from, and it didn't make him feel any better. He promised her mother that this would never happen on his watch.

CHAPTER 27

THIRTY MINUTES EARLIER

The suspicious van circled the block twice before finally making a right turn on an uneven, rocky road. Main Street housed some of the poorest roads in the city. The driver pulled to the side of the curb, and parked near the steps entrance where a curvy brown skinned girl was running up forty flights of stairs that lead to the community park. He spoke through a handheld transceiver. "Everybody in place? The package has arrived." Both driver and passenger were undetectable. They wore hoods, ski mask and gloves behind chalky tented windows.

"Ten-four, we in place," came an unknown voice over a two-way radio - device in an entirely different vehicle. Just then, an older girl appeared. She had sun kissed skin, and a tasty athletic build with alluring legs. She took off down the steps like a bat out of hell. The closer she got, the more tense the men became. They sat upright. It's a remarkable sunny day for such a bold act, but this opportunity would likely never come again. The back door of the van ejects the moment, Ruby's feet touches the bottom. There wasn't a moment to spare. The girl yelled from the top of the steps and near-ly blew their cover. Ruby was forcibly taken fast, tossed inside a waiting van that sped off leaving not a trace.

The Present

"Any tails, are we clear?"

"Nothing we can't handle. Hold tight. Over."

"You asshole!" Ruby snatches off her blindfold livid. Cuddy pulled his mask off and desperately tried not to laugh. So did the driver.

"Did you have to be so rough, dang?"

"You wanted it to look legit, right?" Lil Jay said over his shoulder.

"I can't believe I did that," Ruby says, massaging her neck where Cuddy had applied just a little too much pressure. "Wait, my necklace," Ruby was instantly agitated when she learned that the necklace her dad had given her for her twelfth birthday was missing. She's visibly upset, but Cuddy quickly reassures Ruby that it'll be okay.

"You're such a naughty girl. Come over here." Ruby fell into Cuddy's arms.

"Damn, all this just to see me, girl?"

"They left me no other choice." Ruby lay her head across Cuddy's chest for the remainder of the ride. Except for radios and police scanners, no one said a word for the next ten minutes. Meanwhile, the driver focused on the shake and bake. *Shake and bake* was a system used by the car thieves to lose any unwanted followers. They used various parking decks to switch vehicles, and they always had decoys in place to confuse their pursuers. They had an airtight system. They dumped the van blocks away from where they did the snatch and grab. Cuddy and Ruby exchanged vehicles at least three times until Cuddy was certain he wasn't being followed.

Every local news station in the city was covering Ruby's abduction. Ruby had done unruly things in the past to seek attention, but this time even she knew she'd gone too far. Yet, she didn't care. No one seemed to consider her feelings in all this, so why should she consider theirs? Her friends had been abducted. Why would her parents keep her away from the only person who could bring her joy? *That was a big mistake.* As they laid snuggled up in the bedroom of the spacious condo, Cuddy had never felt better.

Finally, he had his girl all to himself. They had risked everything to be together. Ruby cuts an eye at Cuddy as he laughed out loud. She figured he was just tripping off Chris Tucker acting a fool in Friday. Truthfully, Cuddy was having his own private joke. He'd never done something so outrageous before. If authorities got whiff of their deceitful actions, they'd both be thrown in the slammer and possibly stoned. It was such a shameful act, but they were in love. What else would make someone do something so stupid?

He knew Ruby was still being watched. She was the prize. The organization wanted her. It was his job to make sure it didn't happen. Cuddy had a little short of a half of a million put up. He would use that cash to stay one step ahead of their adversaries. He didn't trust the police. From his short stint with Big Diaz, Cuddy knew a criminal enterprise this lucrative, couldn't operate successfully without cops on the payroll. His biggest fear today was someone intercepting Ruby from him. He couldn't live with himself had things went left. But the plan worked perfectly. Now, returning Ruby home was the task at hand. They hadn't spoken about how long she would be away. But watching her parents carry on the way they did on the news tonight made his stomach turn. He didn't say anything to Ruby, but he was already strategizing her return. "You can never tell anyone about this shit, you hear.... What we did," Cuddy sighs and shakes his head. "It's fucked up on so many levels, Ruby."

"Boy, you scared me, dang."

"Babe, I need you to understand the seriousness of this.

"Cuddy, I do. Are you serious? Ha ha."

"Not a word to your mama or your daddy, ever. We could go to jail. We are taking this to the grave babe."

"No one has ever made me feel the way you do," Ruby voiced softly. She only wanted to savor the rest of the time they had left together. Ruby reassured him that they were on the same page, but that she didn't want to think about it now. With the stunt she'd pulled, there was no telling the next time she'd see Cuddy. Ruby simply wanted to be hugged through the night.

CHAPTER 28

Undisclosed location

A huge Caucasian guy with an enormous pot belly impatiently paces the section behind his desk inside a spacious lavishly decorated office. He stopped when a pair of timid face, police officers walked in. One tall with a rough beard that looked long overdue for a shave. His partner, Hernandez was short and stocky with dingy overalls. He had dark hair and talked with a Spanish accent. The older gentlemen behind the desk glared at both men before ordering them to take a seat.

"How long you two been clocking this Parker girl?"

"Months at least," the men answer in union.

"What do you have to say for yourselves? You surveilled this girl for months and the one chance you get to take her, you let someone else beat you to the punch? Help me understand."

"They were professionals sir." Roger Pete, the taller of the two finally spoke.

"And what are you, amateurs? Because that's what the fuck you're acting like!"

"You had to see it. That's all there is to it." Roger Pete contested.

"They knew we'd be there," Hernandez adds. "They weren't alone."

"I don't give a shit. I have people to answer to. Let me lay down the facts. A half a million bucks is missing. The boyfriend is the only link to our man. I'm upset, I want retribution. But my partners want us to pull out. Its business for them but for me, this shit is personal. Diaz was my guy in this region. Losing him cost me way more than a half a mill. The girl is gone. The cops are involved now. Obviously, we have new competition in town. Snatch the boyfriend. It's time to bring him in. Take some extra men, and don't fuck this up."

CHAPTER 29

Across Town Next Morning

In the middle of morning rush hour traffic, drivers and passengers alike, cling to their seats in shock and awe. Like children watching a horror flick, car horns blew instantaneously. Folks clutched their cell phones. The estrange girl pushed opened the rear door of a luxury black Suburban at the intersection with the most horrifying look on her face. The Suburban rammed the vehicle in front of it to clear a pathway. There was a hint of relief on her face. She stopped momentarily to observe the SUV whip the corner violently. She was half dressed and appeared disoriented. But she didn't stop, she didn't look at anyone. She bolted through the streets like lightening, shifting and dodging in and out of moving traffic .

"WAIT A MINUTE, IS THAT THE GIRL FROM THE NEWS?

"Which one??" A woman says to her husband.

"OMG! Are you okay?"

"Stop, let us help you!" Two VCU College students yell in union.

"Call the police!" Chants a homeless guy on the media strip. The girl had just blew pass him.

"No, the ambulance. She looks hurt. Omg, Poor thing."

They all yell simultaneously. Drivers had pulled to the side of the road. Down the street, a nervous Cuddy took the binoculars from his face, turning to his boy concerned. "Don't worry, she'll be alright." Lil Jay reassured. "Someone will call the police or if not, the police precinct is in walking distance."

"I supposed to made sure she got there at least."

"At what risk though?" Lil Jay asked. "We can't be connected to this shit in no shape, form or fashion"

"True story," Cuddy replies. Lil Jay throws the car in drive and they cruise off in a black Tesla sport.

"She's a block away from the police station, over." A voice comes across the airwaves.

"Keep your distance, but don't let her out of your sight." Cuddy replies. "Over."

"Ten-four."
"Okay," Cuddy breathe a sigh of relief. "We don't have a lot of time. Let's get to the attorney's office.

CHAPTER 30

Attorneys' office

He enters the attorney's office just in time to see ***Breaking News*** flashing across the plasma TV mounted on the wall. "Just in time," The 6'3 towering frame hovers over the boys as they walk in and quickly glue themselves to the TV screen. "Why don't you boys have a seat. How do you know they're after you?"

"Because they snatch my decoy an hour ago thinking he was me. They are only coming for me because my girl got snatched."

"But she was found..." The attorney pauses to read over his notes. "This morning to be exact. Her escape video has surfaced. It's everywhere."

"I saw it," Cuddy replied uninterested. "It's a lot going on counsel. I need you to stay focus. I haven't had a chance to process her getting taken, let alone her escaping the next day. Her parents are keeping shit extra tight. I can't see her or talk to her."

"I understand. So, what is it that you need me to do? You paid me a very handsome retainer's fee. Allow me to earn my money."

"I have evidence that could blow the lid off this whole thing."

"Meaning the sex traffic organization. Whom you worked for a short while. And these same people took your friends and just recently, your girl." Every so often, Lil Jay and Cuddy would exchange concerned looks while the attorney talked.

"That's correct."

"And now they want you?"

"I'm only alive because of what I know, and they think I took their money."

"Well. Did you?"

"No, and it can never be proven."

The attorney glances down at his notes for a few seconds. "And what about this witness who puts you at the scene? Tina?"

Cuddy shrugs his shoulders, "don't know, they say she's missing."

"And let me guess, the police think you're involved?"

"The police say a lot of things, but can't seem to prove shit. The thing is this. They are coming for me. But I don't care, because I'm getting my affairs in order. What I need..." Cuddy breaths a deep sigh. "Is for them to leave my girl alone. And I need you to help me come up with the best strategy to ensure that my plans are carried out. Regardless of what happens to me in the next up-and-coming days. I need you to handle this."

Lil Jay observed his friend with worry upon hearing his statement. The attorney understood the task at hand and got right on the job.

CHAPTER 31

Ruby couldn't stop smiling. She couldn't keep Cuddy out of her head. Though meeting under foolish circumstances, it was the best day of her life. She could still smell his scent, and feel his warmth and gentle embrace. His presence still lingered as though he was now a part of her. Their time together was well worth the shit storm they'd caused. She didn't regret it. In the name of love, she and Cuddy had done the unthinkable. What hurt her the most was keeping her parents in the dark. She had never been so withdrawn from them, and the lies were piling up. But if what she'd done was so heinous, then how come she felt so good? Her mom would never understand her love for Cuddy. And her dad, *well that's another story.*

For now, Ruby had to mask her true feelings and play the battered victim around those who didn't know her truth. The police and Ruby's parents had insisted she be looked over by a physician. Touched or not, Linda pressed for her to go, but Ruby wouldn't hear of it. She only wanted to be home with her family and left alone by everyone else. Ruby being kidnapped was one thing, but her returning home was another. It made Linda sympathize more with the mothers who weren't as fortunate. Like Katrina and Chrystal's moms.

Linda would cringe inside whenever she ran into them. And when Ruby was away, she didn't leave her home once. She couldn't handle the stares and the sympathy from everyone. It would make her reality all too real and Linda couldn't accept Ruby being gone. She thanked God for sparing her that grief. One day without her daughter nearly drove her nuts. And there were many questions. Like where the hell was her baby? Had they hurt her? Was she still in the country? Or God forbid worse, her organs harvested and put on the black market for sale? When she got the news of a video surfacing across social media of Ruby's courageous escape, Linda was happy as a lark. And when she finally saw her girl walk through that door for the first time, she felt an overwhelming feeling of love and gratitude.

She thought of Ruby's friends and their parents as she sat with her daughter in her arms. The police wanted Ruby to make a statement. She was livid with the detective and law enforcement for not protecting Ruby.

Out of the blue, the detective was acting a bit aggressive. He came by the apartment minutes after Ruby arrived. He wanted to speak with her about the kidnappers, and suggested having her placed in protective custody. He even questioned Linda about Cuddy. He wanted to know had Ruby been in contact, but Linda shut him down. She was like a ferocious mama lioness over her cub. She didn't allow anyone to go near Ruby.

The detective was on his way out of the door when Ruby stepped out of her bedroom for the first time, and walked over to the top of the stairs. She had been eavesdropping, but at the mention of Cuddy's name, she couldn't compose herself any longer. The detective noticed Ruby there instantly as if he had been anticipating her. He pulled out a necklace from his inside suit pocket, and dangled the thing in front of them. The detective smirked as she reacted to the necklace her dad brought her. So does Linda. "I thought you'd recognize this."

"Why do you have this?" Linda immediately asked while at the same time relieving the detective of Ruby's necklace. Her actions surprised the detective. Then he got a call that looked to be important.

He turned to Linda. "We're not finish here. Glad to see you back home Ruby." Then he was gone.

CHAPTER 32

It's a normal day inside the city. Behind the murky clouds, thunder and lightning ripped through a spacious blue sky. Residents of the newly renovated *Ward Towers* moved hastily to avoid the obvious downpour that was sure to come. The place was also the home of some would-be investors. They were wolves in sheep clothing. The ruthless band turned out to be criminals. Once a place where vibrant elderly folks kicked back to enjoy and live out their last days comfortably, had metamorphose into a fentanyl apocalypse. The sight was downright pathetic. The city's heroin epidemic was like 1990's crack era turned up to the max.

In numerous cities around the country, clinics were popping up out of the woodworks to combat the growing epidemic. Its shocking to say the least. That the government would provide aid and a facility for addicts to get high off illegal substances. ***What a brave new world.*** Supposedly, the idea was to decrease the overwhelming fentanyl overdoses. Ward Towers had similar issues with their addicts. Five deaths in one month's time, certainly warranted upgrades or a complete transformation to the way the place was ran. Following the governments lead, the criminals quickly carved out a few sections inside the high riser to make it more accommodating. The addicts were now able to buy their drugs and get high all in one place, and there was not a single overdose afterwards.

Big Diaz had reached his pinnacle in the heroin distribution trade. He knew that after five fentanyl overdoses, an investigation was sure to come. And he wasn't about to wait around for the inevitable. The most unexpected thing happened. While slowly making his transition, a new unlikely opportunity presented itself. It couldn't have come at a more perfect time. The group had supposedly been watching him for some time and admired the strong hold he held over certain compartments in the city.

Big Diaz reluctantly joined on to the band. Like fentanyl, the gig was a shameful occupation that he didn't want to be openly associated with. He even created a cover to hide his foulness. The clubs and the dancers were all a front for the sex trafficking business. But he did it and made his overseers a shit load of cash. Once he was in, there was no turning back. He saw his first million bucks as a result of selling girls. He figured that if he didn't do it, they'd simply find another unsavory hoodlum to get it done. Big Diaz hit an all time low. He was the worse kind of race trader. He used his clout and years of connections made in the dope trade to lure in his prey. He took the oath to never ask questions. His employers existed in the shadows only, as if they didn't exist, yet they were everywhere.

Melanated girls were at risk, especially those who Big Diaz knew personally. This put him and his former street associates at odds. For some of them, what Big Diaz had done was worse than selling dope. And many of them wanted no parts of it. Big Diaz was ousted from the click. Despite their frustration toward their friend, nothing in the world could have prepared them for the news of Big Diaz's death. And it wasn't long before Cuddy's name turned up. It had been rumored that Cuddy was the last person with Big Diaz before he met his demise. And to top it off, the only witness that could put Cuddy at the scene, was reportedly missing. So not only were the police interested in Cuddy, but threats were coming back to him from Big Diaz' s people. They felt Cuddy at least owed them a sit down. But to give them what they wanted, would be admitting that he did something wrong. Cuddy had to play it smart. The walls were beginning to close in on him. There were some who wanted to hear him out, and unfortunately, there were others who simply wanted to put Cuddy's head to bed.

CHAPTER 33

A shooter has him marked thirty yards out. A kid plays near the entrance of the vast three-story high riser. He alerts everyone through a handheld device as the Luxury Lincoln turns on the block and drives by them. A youngster on over-watch who sat by a window on one of the top floors couldn't have been no more than eighteen. He took aim out the window,

"It's Cuddy, want me to split his shit?"

"Nah, take out the front tire," came the command from over his shoulder. The youngster who went by the name of Tee Bone, channeled his breathing while staring through the scope of his rifle. Then he fired a single shot.

Thirty minutes earlier
The silver SUV pulls into an empty parking deck under a Hilton Inn hotel just minutes outside the city. Lil Jay is inside a black SUV with the engine running. He's up and out of the truck the minute Cuddy appears.

"Bad fucking idea, you're not doing it!" Lil Jay protested. "Why you going all out for this girl mane?"

"Watch your mouth." Cuddy says and sighs. "Besides, I don't have much of a choice. They're holding the homey and won't let him go unless I show up. I gotta align myself up with some real niggas."

"But you can't trust them."

"I know bro." Cuddy sighs again and leans against the SUV. He looked exhausted. The last thing he wanted to do was go around Big Diaz's little brother Ant. These guys were shady and given the history between them, Lil Jay was right that Cuddy shouldn't trust them. It was a stupid idea. To go behind enemy lines knowing the circumstances. Big Diaz caught a bad break, but it was time for his people to know that it wasn't Cuddy's fault. And how the hell could they come up with something so ridicules. Cuddy was a car thief and had no business associating himself with the likes of little Ant, and his band of evil, fentanyl assassins. But the corner he'd been backed into left him no choice. They had his boy. Cuddy was in over his head and knew it. What could he have been thinking to go and work for someone like Big Diaz? Many times, he tried to think back on how it all started.

Cuddy would never have stumbled across the photos of Ruby and their friends if he hadn't worked for Big Diaz. He finally understood his position. The information he possessed was powerful, incriminating even. Cuddy had evidence that could bring down a multi billion-dollar criminal enterprise. He alluded them for as long as he could, but he knew that eventually their money and resources would catch up with him. *Like now.* His boy had been gone for twenty-four hours.

"Its risky I know, but I know what I'm doing."

"It's too much of a risk bro." Lil Jay was worried. "We're nothing like them. I don't get it. They could kill you."

"Just trust me. If things go left, you know what to do. For now, just have my back."

CHAPTER 34

Shirtless thugs swarm Cuddy's vehicle after it collides with a parked car. The front tire on the drivers side was dismantled. He was swiftly blindfolded and roughed up by Big Diaz's, gangster baby brother and his crew. They escorted him into a section of the high riser. Once Cuddy was inside and the blindfold was taken off his eyes, he found Big Diaz's little brother Ant standing before him.

"I kicked your ass the last time I saw you," Ant remarks and points a finger at Cuddy's face. You got a lot of explaining to do. What the fuck are you doing here lil nigga?"

As Cuddy struggled to regain consciousness and adjust his eyes to the lightening in the room, images of the altercation between Ant and his goons resurfaced. Truth be told, Cuddy had left a good impression on Ant for taking the beaten for his boys that day. It had been rumored that Big Diaz's people were in the streets looking for him behind, Big Diaz's demise. If he didn't make the right move, this could end bad for Cuddy. He thought of every possible angle.

"I don't know what you heard, but I ain't have shit to do with what happen to the big homey. But I know who did. And because of what I know, they been fucking with me ever since. They're holding Dennis right now to exchange for me."

"Who the fuck are THEY?" Ant appeared suspicious, but Cuddy had captured his undivided attention.

"The motherfuckers your brother worked for. That's who killed him. You know what Big Diaz was into. The people who run that shit is responsible. And now they wanna see me. They have my boy. I must get him back, but I can't go in alone. I need your help Ant."

"And why would I get involved with some hot shit like that?"

"I'm the same lil nigga you watched grow up. Big Diaz worked for these people, and they killed him for reasons I don't know about. Now I ain't asking you to do shit, but have my back. This is business." Ant was quiet for a while as he observed the guys around him growing restless. Dennis was a well-known pane in the ass, yet he was loved by many, especially the dealers.

"Maybe this will help you decide." Cuddy pulls out a knot of cash from his inside coat pocket. Take it, I don't have much time." The guys hanging around were like hungry hounds. "Oh shit, this lil nigga strapped." The words roll off Ant's tongue. Everyone appeared shocked to see Cuddy with the cash. The last they checked, Cuddy and his boys were just local car thieves.

"Damn lil cuz, how mu-"

"It's fifty thousand," Cuddy answers, tossing the cash to Ant.

"Why don't I just kill you myself and take the money. Why even bother with the rest of this bullshit you bringing me."

"For two reasons," Cuddy replies. "One, I didn't come here alone. My ride is outside waiting." Its then that Ant notices the earpiece in Cuddy's ear. Lil Jay had just alerted him that he was on site. "And two," Cuddy goes on.   "That's 50k Ant, what sense would it make to kill me? I've always known you to be a stand-up dude. Plus, I feel like I did you a solid. Even though your niggas nearly killed me."

"You got a vest on my nigga?" Ant asked Cuddy out of nowhere. It didn't register when Cuddy opened his jacket to give him the cash. But he saw it then. Cuddy was a little guy and the vest added on a few pounds. "Damn my nigga, you not playing are you?"

"I'm in a jam bro."

"You did do me a solid. I appreciate you coming thru. You know my niggas. They ready for whatever. So, what's the plan?"

A look of relief sweeps across Cuddy's face for the first time since he arrived. "I thought you'd never fucking ask."

CHAPTER 35

"Hey man, listen. I don't know anything about what you're talking about or what you do. Or why you would even take my friend. We steal cars and I helped Big Diaz out a few times, but anything else Big Diaz had going on, I knew nothing about. I only worked for Big Diaz because I needed the extra money. My mama would kill me if she knew I was working in a strip club. Now please, let my boy go. His family is worried, and I don't want them to involve the police."

"Is that a threat?" Boss hog growled.

"No sir, it's not. Just facts."

"And who else knows that you're here?"

"Well, I wouldn't dare come here alone."

"A real wise ass I see. My people saw you that night you know. At the bartender's place, you were there. You wanna know how I know that?"

"I have no idea what you mean."

"Listen asshole." Boss hog exhales smoke from his cigar and points his chunky finger at Cuddy.

"We have surveillance photos of you casing the girl's joint. I know this because my men were watching her place. And then she mysteriously goes missing?" Theres a pause. He awaits a response, but Cuddy doesn't budge, which infuriates Boss hog even more. He grits his teeth and in a calmer tone, he says, "what do you think the police would do with that? I could end you. Now where the fuck is my money?"

"Boss, you might wanna look at this." A guy yells, standing near the window. The new discovery shook Cuddy to the core. He could recall that night clearly. Lil Jay rambled on and on about a suspicious vehicle, tailing them after leaving Tina's place. It was the first time, Cuddy didn't feel in control of his ordeal. And he dreaded the thought of someone holding incriminating evidence over his head. Tina was buried, and Cuddy worried about it in his mind, especially after the encounter with Boss hug. What exactly did they see? How many other times was he caught out of pocket like the night at Tina's? Another important factor struck him as he sat there in the hot seat awaiting his fate.

Why was Boss hog interested in the bartender anyway? Cuddy heard the very same words spoken from the detective's mouth. His only conclusion was that he was being played and lined up by Boss hog and a corrupt detective. That fact alone horrified him. He was afraid for Ruby. Her parents worked closely with the detective. No matter what though, he remained cool. Cuddy couldn't allow these hounds to smell his fear. They whispered intensely amongst themselves as they gathered near the window of the room.   "Who the fuck are these assholes?" Cuddy heard Boss hog spew angrily at his guys.

"This shit is becoming a fucking circus boss," another man in the room says.

"Hey asshole, you know anything about this?" Boss hog yells over at Cuddy.

Cuddy responds. "It's like I said before. My boy needs to be released. His people are worried."

"You did keep your word," Boss hog answers back stubbornly... "And a deal is a deal."

Deep sigh, Boss hog stands by the window fuming with anger. Things were intensifying outside and it worried him. They had too much at stake. Bare chested males, shouted obscenities and pointed assault rifles toward their building. One phone call, he could have the bastards arrested and thrown in the slammer, or put down like dogs if they resisted. This was all so beneath him. He was told by his associates to leave this issue alone months ago. Boss hog thought his intimidation tactics would scare the kid into coughing up the stolen cash. But Cuddy had proven himself to be a bit craftier than the good fellas had predicted. Cuddy and his friend, Dennis was released without incident.

CHAPTER 36

THREE MONTHS LATER

She had a unique side to tell. Ruby's story had gained her national attention. She'd been kidnapped, and returned unscathed. Because sex trafficking was a serious matter, the city wanted to hear from her. Very few girls went through such an ordeal and lived to talk about it. She received numerous invitations to visit schools and colleges. The spotlight had become overwhelming for Ruby.

She wanted her old life back. Many people were excited and encouraged her to walk into her destiny. Ruby only cared what Cuddy thought. With all the chaos and media hype, Cuddy seemed to have fallen off the grid. She hadn't heard a word from him in over a week and Ruby worried. The last time they spoke, Cuddy appeared apprehensive. He told her that their nightmare was almost over. He explained that once the dust settled, things would go back to normal for her. Though the news reassured Ruby, she was concerned about his choice of words. Wouldn't they both be alright when the dust settled?

Its Linda's day off. So she's in the kitchen cleaning, lighting her candles and doing her laundry. She simply would not sit down. Truth be told, it was a form of her therapy. These past few weeks had been a roller coaster ride. She was having a difficult time adjusting to the new wave of attention. She worried about so many things. Ruby had so many opportunities before her, but Linda feared the pressure could be too much for Ruby to bare. Something was up with Ruby and Linda didn't know what. She seemed distant. Linda could only imagine the trauma Ruby suffered. And just this past week, Latasha Edwards, a longtime friend of Ruby ever since grade school, overdosed off Fentanyl.

She was an athlete like Ruby. The poor girl didn't stand a chance. Latasha's idiot, dope dealing cousins left a blender at the house that was used to mix up dope and fentanyl. Instead of trashing it, the doe doe younger cousin let it soak in hot water. Her eyes lit up at the mere sight of the expensive blender. Latasha anxiously mixed her fruit inside the blender like always.

The poor girl never knew what hit her. She sipped her smoothie delightfully and halfway through, Latasha passed out on the couch beside her grandmother. She died right there inside her grandmothers living room. Even with family members present, she couldn't be saved because Latasha's condition was unknown.

The fentanyl crisis had taken out a great deal of decent people. The city was under attack. Linda worried about Ruby running to drugs for an escape, and the thought alone shook her to the core. But could she really blame her if she did? Linda lost sleep thinking about Latasha and the sickening way she died. She wanted Ruby to excel in life.

Linda noticed the trash bin full. She caught herself about to yell for Ruby to come down and do her chores. Instead, she decided it'll take less effort and energy on her part, if she simply dumped the trash herself. *This time.* Once it was done, she would certainly sit down.

Outside, Linda opened the lid on the garbage bin. She was seconds away from tossing the garbage inside when she caught sight of something startling. She noticed the tip of it sticking out from the bag of trash dumped the day before. Linda appeared stunned for a moment, confused even. But when she came to, she didn't think twice. Linda grabbed the object from the trash bin.

CHAPTER 37

SIX MONTHS EARLIER

Cuddy and the last of the girls had just arrived at Delightful Lounge. He'd been running back and forth all day, from the bus station to the airport and back to the night club. When another load of girls arrived, Cuddy was back on the highway punching it. Cuddy and his crew were so efficient in how they committed their auto thefts, and transported the girls around town, that Big Diaz brought them on permanently. Big Diaz had girls pouring in from as far as Huston Texas, and Cuddy was there at the desired location to collect them. Cuddy was exhausted to say the least. He wanted nothing more than to put distance between himself and this club. The pay was great, but it left such a weighty burden on his soul.

Dope dealing was one thing, but this sex trafficking business was the ultimate work of the devil. Cuddy was just a small fish swimming with gigantic whales and vicious sharks. His motivation was love, and bringing to halt whatever sadistic plan they had for Ruby. There were many layers to the organization. The things Cuddy heard about what happened to the girls he met were atrocious. Some girls were shipped to foreign countries to be debased into sex slaves, others met even worse fates. Like their organs harvested and sold on the black market.

Cuddy shared in the guilt. The only thing that kept him from going completely insane, was the fact that he had a purpose. Ruby was the love of his young life. He knew without a doubt that he'd go all out for her, even if it meant risking his own life to save hers. The ordeal changed Cuddy in many ways. Were they even aware of Cuddy's knowledge? ***Keep your enemies close?*** Cuddy wasn't sure. He could barely stomach being around Big Diaz. It was a dangerous game to play, but the risk was worth the reward. If it meant keeping Ruby safe, Cuddy was all in. He began down the corridor where Big Diaz and Kenny are usually inside the office around this hour, sorting out the money to pay their employees. He was anxious to just get his cash and go. Cuddy startled Felisha, the bar tender as she exited the rest room just as Cuddy was passing by. Cuddy says hello and smiles inside at her there shaken.

"I should fuck you up for scaring me like that boy."

"I didn't mean too," Cuddy says with a smooth smile. Then shouting from the conference room ahead put Cuddy on high alert. He came to a halt outside the room just as Kenny yelled, *how the fuck was I supposed to know she was pregnant?"*

"It's your job to know KP. I don't take in pregnant girls. They're too fuckin' needy and high maintenance. Put her ass on a bus and send her home. These bitches need to be vetted from here on out. No pregnant hoes." Big Diaz was adamant.

"I got it." Little is said between the men as Cuddy grab his cash and go. A few hours later, he's unexpectedly summoned back to the club. Cuddy knew that Big Diaz suspected him. Perhaps even they were aware of the missing photo, Cuddy lifted from their duffel bag. At any rate, none of it mattered now. Back at home, Cuddy began to devise a plan to free Ruby from these bastard's grip for good.

Later that night at dinner
Cuddy speaking, "I don't know about this Lil Jay, this is way the fuck out there man. What the fuck could Ruby be thinking?" Cuddy was vexed.

"It's a brilliant idea!" Lil Jay remarks. "Just think about it. You said it yourself."

"What are you saying? This is the dumbest, most reckless shit I've ever heard of."

"You're saying that because you are only looking at it if it goes wrong." Cuddy was completely against Ruby's plot to fake her own kidnapping. It was just too risky given the circumstances. It was a stupid idea.

"How else are you going to see her? She under lock and key right now, so the snatch and grab gotta be dramatic. And you gotta be around her for the plan to work, right." A smile stretches wide across Lil Jay's face. "We could pull this shit off bro. The crew."

Cuddy pushes Lil Jay playfully and says, "listen to you sounding like a professional kidnapper." Both men laugh endlessly lightening the mood.

"But you're right. It must be drastic. "I'm following now," Cuddy says finally realizing what Lil Jay meant.

"It's a great idea," Lil Jay goes on excited. "You just didn't think of it. She gets to see you, and you get to kill two birds with one stone."

"True story my brother. You ain't never lied." Cuddy smiles for the first time. It was certainly a load off. Indeed, Cuddy had a plan. The damn thing just had to work.

CHAPTER 38

Cuddy seemed to be well rested in orange jail overalls. He's escorted over to the conference table where Det Destiny waited. "Well, did you hear?" The detective says the minute, Cuddy took his seat. Cuddy shrugged his shoulders unbothered.

"I didn't detective. But you would know that since you kidnapped me."

"Don't be so dramatic. On another note... The bartender, Tina." The detective delay to get a read on Cuddy's reaction. Just the mention of the bartender surely got Cuddy's attention. "Well, it appears that her body was discovered this morning. It's been all over the news. Good news right." He wanted to see Cuddy squirm. Det. Destiny worked for Boss hog, Cuddy was certain of it now. He was a part of their team here trying to score points at Cuddy's expense.

"Of course, that's excellent news detective," Cuddy says trying his hardest not to appear affected. Cuddy wasn't in the best mode. He was arrested and held without charges. His location was undisclosed to the public. They wanted Cuddy on lock and key while they went after Ruby. The organization hadn't forgotten about Ruby and Cuddy, outsmarting them and stealing over a half million of their cash. They wanted another crack at Ruby. Boss hog and his partners were defiant, as well as their illustrious customers. They were gearing up to snatch, Ruby and expected for their boys in blue to assist in making it happen.

Their client, an Iranian Prince from a country several hundred miles away had requested the young beauty. The foreigner was willing to pay a healthy price for Ruby in her purest form. It's clear now why Boss hog went against his partners to see the deal through. One million US currency is what the prince offered for Ruby, and Boss hog wasn't leaving that money on the table. Plus, he wanted to stick it to Cuddy. If the kid wasn't coughing up the cash, then they'd take the next best thing, and make a million bucks in the process. They had leverage over Cuddy and resources to crush him.

"Does Ruby and her parents know you're working for the same people that wants to take her.”

“That a be you sir.” Det. Destiny replies.

“I was wired the last time I met with you know who. You know who I mean. Let him know. I had a hidden camera on. We have his face. We can identify him. If you kill me, this entire enterprise that you’re a part of my man crumbles. My attorneys are holding on to it in case you pulled some stupid shit like this.”

“You think you’re smart.”

“I’m trying to survive, it’s a difference.”

“Get comfortable Cuddy. You’re not going home.”

“This shit illegal. What am I being charged with?”

“For being a smart ass right now.”

A knock at the window got the detective out of his seat. When the room was empty, panic gripped Cuddy like never before. He slammed his fist down hard against the table. The cops were fucking with him, they had to be. Their plan for his life began to unfold. They ran down on him at 3:00 am, and had been holding him for two days. He realized that he could be killed and never heard from again. Perhaps that would be best. This news about the bartender had him on pins and needles. If linked to Tina’s murder, things would end bad for him. Tina’s remains being found could put a monkey wrench in his whole plan.

Cuddy informed his people when things got real for him, he would never go missing without warning. And if he did, assume the worse. Cuddy’s attorney even suggested in a meeting once that he be injected with a tracking device. The idea sounded absurd at first and Cuddy dismissed it instantly. But now, he wished he hadn’t. The attorney warned him that he was in over his head, and that he should use every precaution at his disposal. He knew he was being monitored. On the outside, Cuddy remained normal, but inside, he was a ball of confusion. As he sat there in his thoughts, it dawned on him that he’d been preparing for a drastic event. He hired a financial consultant to assist him in a couple lucrative investments. He owned two properties and was able to put money aside for Ruby. He had one last card to play. And if it worked, just maybe there was a little light at the end of the tunnel after all. *Maybe*

CHAPTER 39

Ruby is staring at her reflection in the full-length mirror when her mom storms into her room unannounced. Before Ruby could react, Linda had already saw what Ruby had been hiding. "I don't have to guess who this belongs to anymore, now do I?" Linda holds out the pregnancy test heart broken. The hurt and betrayal leaked out of each word she spoke. Ruby is frozen there with her hand on her baby bump. She stared at the test in a trance unable to utter one word.

"Ruby, I don't understand. How are you pregnant? I thought you were a virgin. Pregnant Ruby? What the fuck is going on? I'm calling your dad right now." Linda says and was on her way out of the door when Ruby interjected.

"Wait mama." Ruby takes a deep breath. "I was ashamed. I didn't wanna relive what happen to me mama."

"What happen to you? I'm confused. What happen baby?? Please, I need to know." Linda begged.

We must take this lie to the grave, Ruby. You can't tell a soul.' Cuddy's warning played over and over in her head. No one could find out about their union. *'Not even your mama. Now promise me.'* She only wanted to protect Cuddy, so she finally said it out loud.

"I was raped mama."

"OMG! But you said nothing ha-"

"I was ashamed, and I didn't know how to talk about it. Not even to you mama."

"Why didn't you go to the doctor in the beginning and let them look over you, Ruby?"

"I don't want to be anybody's victim. I don't want people looking at me and judging me. I still don't. And the police have never been on our side. So, I'm not telling them anything."

"Cuddy right. He's got you thinking that the cops are not right. So, what are your plans, Ruby?"

"My plans are to prepare to be a mother, I guess."

"Have your rapist baby? Do you really think that's the best decision?"

"It's my baby, mama. I didn't ask for this to happen to me. And this baby didn't ask to be born. I won't abort it."

Tears replace words and in minutes, they are loving on one another. And despite the circumstances, Linda was proud of Ruby's strength. To harbor such an ugly secret for as long as she did, spoke volumes. Linda didn't like it. It wasn't the plan she envisioned for her daughter. She felt responsible for not protecting Ruby. All she simply wanted to do now was support her. Ruby shouldn't have to bear this burden alone. Suddenly, every telephone in their home began to ring. There was a firm knock at the front door. Ruby turned to her mom with confusion plastered across her face.

"Did you call dad?"

"No. Answer the phone while I get the door." Ruby picked the phone up while her mom rushed to the front door.

"Wait, what?" Did you say Christal? When, where... how?" Ruby drops the phone and erupts into tears. Linda reenters the bedroom out of breath.

"We must get down to the hospital. Its Christal...they found Christal, alive." Linda was so anxious to leave that she hadn't notice Ruby there crying. Obviously, she was alerted about Christal. They were downstairs in a flash. But at the sight of Det. Destiny sitting in their living room, Ruby froze up.

"The detective will escort us to the hospital," Linda says upon reaching the bottom of the stairs, but Ruby's fearful expression concerned her mother. Cuddy didn't trust the detective, so naturally, Ruby didn't trust him either. The detective said he knew they'd be excited to hear the news. He thought he'd deliver it, and offer them a personal escort down to the hospital to see Christal. Ruby reluctantly agreed, and lagged slowly behind her mother out onto the front porch where they found Ruby's dad driving up. He parked in front of the detectives unmarked police car. Ruby took off toward her dad's ride and jumped in the passenger seat of the Chevy Suburban. Linda rode with the detective.

CHAPTER 40

The city had a lot to be thankful for. The news story of Christal had spread far and wide. Then there was the highlighted special of all three girls. The news pundit spoke about them being friends, hinting at the trio possibly being targets. They focused on the fact that two of the three girls had come back home. Doctors examined Christal's condition. She'd been abused and raped several times. She tested positive for two separate STD's. She was discovered at an abandon bus stop, not far from the Medical Center.

A homeless couple whose bench Christal borrowed, saw her and quickly pulled over a police cruiser riding by. She was drugged, beaten and dehydrated, unrecognizable to anyone who knew her. Authorities identified Christal and contacted her mom. Christal's return was a media circus. Everyone from the police department, media and her family wanted to hear from her. But Christal wasn't talking to anyone. Her vital signs had leveled and she was completely conscious. Her mom put a pen and pad by her bedside for her whenever she was ready to talk.

Ruby arrived with her dad, who had to serve as her buffer from the flashing cameras and mics being shoved in her face. "Two down, one to go Ruby. Katrina will be back next, what do you say?"

"No comment!" Ruby's dad answered back to the aggressive reporter as they rushed down the corridor. Linda and Det. Destiny followed close behind, arriving at the elevator. It's a short ride up. The lobby was a mixture of Christal's family members and law enforcement. But other people were there, faces Ruby didn't recognize, and it made her nervous.

Where the hell was Cuddy? She needed him right now. And it struck her as odd that Cuddy was still a no show with Christal's return. His voice mail picked up on the first ring, and his aunt hadn't seen or heard a word from him in weeks. It didn't sit well with her that she couldn't contact Cuddy when she needed to. His absence made her feel unsafe. Ruby clinched her father's hand as they moved around the lobby. Suddenly, Christal's mom appeared. She and the doctor stood outside of the lobby, but the minute she noticed Ruby and her parents standing there, she shot over to greet them. She gently took Ruby by the hand and said, "come quickly, Ruby. I'm so happy you're here. Christal wants to see you. She's not talking to anyone, but she ask for you." The woman smiled through her tears while trying to bring Ruby up to speed about her daughter's condition. Linda and Ruby's dad, Roger went back with her. Everyone else looked on confused, others agitated and impatient for an update about Christal's condition.

Ruby hesitated before entering Christal's room. She didn't really know what to expect. Christal's mom stepped aside and waited for Ruby to walk in. Christal was facing the door when Ruby entered. Everyone else hung back behind the door. When they're finally alone, Ruby notices the note pad beside Christal that read, ***I wanna see Ruby.***

"I thought I'd never see ya'll again." Christal gave a weary sigh. She looked exhausted. Ruby cringed at the horrific sight of her.

"But I thought you couldn't talk." Ruby said, giving Christal a soothing hug.

"I can talk. Just didn't feel like talking." Christal kept her tone low and her eyes would occasionally dart nervously over at the glass window where her mom and Ruby's parents waited. Occasionally, a detective would pop up to look in on Christal. The girls hugged and they cried together, but then Christal's paranoia became obvious, drawing suspicion from Ruby. She casted a glance over her shoulder to check on her parents. They were occupied talking. Ruby turned back to Christal excited, taking her hand and placing it on her belly bump. At the same time, Christal glanced up to notice a man outside her door. The creepy sight of him terrified her.

Arrangements had been made for Ruby to be taken tonight. Christal didn't know when or how it would go down, but she was certain that it would happen. The guy noticed, Christal joyfully caressing Ruby's stomach, and his dissatisfaction was unquestionable. Christal feverishly watched the door as the color all but drains from her face. Then out of nowhere, Christal blurts out, "they're gonna kill me. You gotta help me."

The comment caught Ruby off guard, leaving her blown away. She was instantly shook.

Christal goes on. "The day they took me, they really wanted you. They took Katrina and then me, but it's you they wanted the whole time."

The fear tightened in Ruby's gut. It laced up through each nerve in her spine and twisted her face into a contortion.

"What are you talking about? And how do you know this?"

"The truth is…" Christal cries. "I haven't been a good friend to you, Ruby. They described you as untouched, rare and pure… And that someone would pay a lot of money for you. They were gonna keep me. I told them that I could help them get you. The only reason I'm here now, is to lure you out. So that they can take you." As Ruby listened, she questioned how they could be friends so long, and she not be aware of Christal's treachery. Ruby wanted to smack the taste out Christal's mouth. This was the ultimate betrayal. Christal had no shame and her jealous edge hadn't gone unnoticed. It was disappointing to say the least. Had Katrina fallen victim to the same fate? ***Betrayal by a lying bitch of a friend.*** Memories flash through her head of them as kids. But looking at Christal now and becoming aware of her vicious plot, Ruby finally understood that their friendship was one sided.

"I'm sorry Ruby."

"Are you really?" Linda enters the room with a look of concern. Ruby doesn't look good.

"What is it?" She asked.

"I'm not safe mama, I need to get out of here.

"What?" Linda appeared perplexed.

"Now, mama! Sorry. I'm gonna vomit."

"Okay babe, let's go." Christal took Ruby by the hand before she could walk away. She let go of Ruby's hand and started to caress her stomach.

"I'm the only one who's not safe, Ruby. This here is your ticket girl. You're good now, Ruby."

Linda looked from Christal to Ruby. She was absolutely dumbfounded. She had so many questions, yet she didn't speak.

A light bulb goes off in Ruby's head. Christal had just confirmed Cuddy's promise to her. ***'In the end, you will be good.'*** Cuddy never included himself, and she wondered just what he truly meant. Where was he and why had no one heard a word from him? Promptly, she had a strong urge to see him. Christal took Ruby by the hand again, snapping her out of her forlorn daze. Christal pulled Ruby closer, whispering, ***"the police are involved. Don't trust them."***

Another conformation that Cuddy was right. After all that was revealed, Ruby still felt pity for Christal. She couldn't bring herself to completely hate her. They were best friends since little girls. She didn't want to see anything else bad happen to her, yet Ruby couldn't see them ever being close again. She was quickly learning that in life, things change and oftentimes, so does the people in your life. Ruby had never been so happy to have her dad by her side. She clung to him as they brushed through a herd of suits, uniforms and hungry reporters.

CHAPTER 41

TWO MONTHS LATER

Today was gender reveal. Talk about nervous, Ruby was on pins and needles. She'd fallen in love with the new life growing inside her, yet horrified altogether. She didn't want to give birth to a daughter who could grow up to one day be a target. The thought alone was crippling. She never imagined having to go through her pregnancy without Cuddy. She hadn't heard anything from him in months. What happen to their plan? Why hadn't anyone reached out to her to make sure she was okay? It was the strangest thing.

Cuddy not being here was not in the plan. After the visit with Christal some months back, Ruby had her mom help break the news to her father. Ruby felt so bad and regretful for misleading her parents in that way. They would never understand the bond between her and Cuddy. In her heart, she truly felt that she made the right choice. And perhaps later in life, Ruby may get the nerve to confess to her parents what truly happen. But it would have to be later. Dad took the news hard. It was the first time she saw him cry. Its what made her secret hard to bare. To watch her parents suffer was gut wrenching, and made her physically weak. Nevertheless, Ruby vowed to stick to the script unless, Cuddy said otherwise.

She had to stay the course. Ruby hid her pregnancy for as long as she could, but now that she was showing, soon came the questions and scrutiny. No one knew her story, which made it easy for them to pass judgment. But Ruby could care less, and purposely let people assume what they wanted. And for those bold enough to inquire about the father of her baby, Ruby would say silly things like, ***I'm something like the virgin, Mary. My baby is special.***

Speaking of babies, Ruby was elated after leaving the doctor's office. She was giving birth to a healthy baby boy. While talking with her mother outside the doctor's office, Ruby perked up. She keyed in on a guy parked in the second row in the far corner. Was she still a target? Ruby thought a detective perhaps because of the suit. He appeared to be monitoring the building. Ruby remained vigilant, alerting her mom to what was happening. Ironically, she recognized the man as he got out of his vehicle and started walking briskly toward them. When he was closer, Ruby's heart fluttered. The stranger happened to be Cuddy's attorney. He was a white man, tall and slender with a receiving hair line. He and Ruby met brief once, but had never had a formal introduction. His name was Richard Hart. He apologized for not contacting, Ruby sooner. He showed them both his identification and in the same instant, he noticed the elephant in the room. He smiled. "I guess a congratulations are in order."

"Thank you," Ruby answers bashfully.

"Would you like to see him?"

"Who? Cuddy?"

"He wants me to bring you to him right away." Mr. Hart checked his watch. "We would have to leave now. I thought you guys would never come out of the doctor's office." Linda wasn't comfortable letting Ruby out of her sight, so she allowed her to leave with the attorney, but followed behind them. They reached their destination within a matter of minutes.

As they're driving along the narrow street, the county jail and its tall barb wire fence comes into view. Ruby turns to the attorney in shock as they turn into the jail parking lot. "CUDDY'S IN JAIL?" Richard Hart faces her with a sympathetic smile.

"Unfortunately, he is. I want to give him a chance to explain. Come on." Richard Hart quickly exited the truck and rounded to Ruby's side of the vehicle. The minute he opened the door, Ruby doubled over and commenced to puking out her lunch on the neatly manicured lawn. The attorney had a look of panic on his face. Linda had been sitting inside her car when she spotted her daughter slumped over. It nearly shook the life out of her. She yelled at Richard Hart as she tended to Ruby. "What the fuck happen to her? What did you do?" Linda was ferocious.

"Absolutely nothing ma'am." The attorney was appalled.

"No mama, its okay. I'm just a little upset is all."

"Why are we here?" Linda turned to the attorney and asked.

"Because Cuddy's here ma."

"Oh hell no. You ain't going into nobody's damn jail."

"My client will be very disappointed if she doesn't show up." The attorney explained that it had to be now. They had to go to the front desk to register. Ruby used wipes from her purse to clean up. Then with the attorney by her side, they shoot up to the jail's entrance. Once they made it to the back where inmates could be seen entering the visitation room, Ruby could feel herself becoming anxious. She thought that Cuddy had abandon her. Attorney Richard Hart pulls out a pack of gum from his inside suit pocket.

"I bet you could appreciate one of these right now," the attorney remarks with a smile. Ruby and Mr. Hart shared a good laugh. He couldn't have been further from the truth. After her accident outside, the gum was refreshing and just what she needed.

On the opposite side of the lobby behind the control booth, the door to the visitation room opens slowly. At least five guys walk through when she sees a familiar face that appeared at least ten pounds lighter. Cuddy did a double take as he entered and saw Ruby standing in the lobby with Mr. Hart. So mesmerized by Ruby's appearance, the jail deputy ushered Cuddy forward for holding up the line.

The visitation room had at least six booths inside. The emotion in his chest choked him up. This day, he had fantasized about for many nights. His reaction to her belly bump was priceless. Once they're sitting across from one another, he was overwhelmed by feelings. The wave of emotions flowing from Cuddy, touched Rudy profoundly. And its only then that it dawns on Ruby, the true meaning behind Cuddy's intentions.

Ruby brought him up to speed about Christal. And Cuddy told Ruby about the corrupt detective and how he lied about finding, Tina's body. Truthfully, it was Christal who had reappeared. The detective was only trying to shake Cuddy up. Ruby told Cuddy about the lie she told her parents. This news shocked Cuddy.

"Are you serious? You did not tell your parents that! Ruby, you got hella nerve girl."

"How else was I supposed to protect you? I couldn't admit to you being the baby's father. Who knows what the detective would try and do with that, being that I'm underage and all."

"Right..." Cuddy remarks. "Good point."

"I guess I'm just crazy in love with you." Ruby sincerely admitted.

"Yeah, our love unlimited. Dope shit!" Cuddy agrees.

There wasn't much time to spare. But Ruby was so lovely. For a minute, Cuddy sat with the phone to his ear, tears flowing and he didn't care about being clowned about it later. Ruby was so relieved to see him, but con-fused at the same time. She had so many questions and concerns. "What's wrong, aren't you happy to see me?" Rudy asked.

"I didn't think I'd ever see you again."

"But why are you here, Cuddy?"

"Because they weren't gonna allow me to just walk away."

Cuddy informed Ruby that he and all his boys were kidnapped at the same time and taken in the middle of the night. They were all tortured and treated foul while in custody for months with no communication. Cuddy admitted to Ruby that though, he didn't openly say it, he never planned to come out of this untouched. "I only wanted to protect you, Ruby. That's the only reason I kept working for Big Diaz. It's how I learned about their plan babe, from working on the inside."

"I'm sorry I doubted you, Cuddy. You put it all on the line for me. I love you so much. I just wish you could be here with me. I mean with us," Ruby emphasized while caressing her stomach.

"I wish I could be there too. I was willing to pay whatever price I had to pay for you to be free, Ruby. Because of your pregnancy, they won't ever bother you again. I got evidence that incriminates them. It's the only rea-son I'm still alive. My attorney cut a deal with the prosecutor for me to be locked up no longer than 36 months. In exchange, the prosecution agreed to drop their investigation and any potential charges against me. This time I gotta do is just their way of fucking me for the money that went missing."

"And you're okay with that? With being away from us for that long."

"It's a small price to pay for love, Ruby. We beat the odds." Cuddy stared deeply into her eyes as the five minute warning was announced.

"Now all we gotta do is get married." His words brought a huge smile to Ruby's face. "I have a few properties already, but the house we're gonna be living in is being built from the ground up. And I put money away for you and the baby."

"You put money away for the baby, but how did you even know that there would be a baby, Cuddy?"

"Because I had the faith of a muster seed, Ruby. And a plan. And love, well love is a mother fucker." Cuddy and the rest of the prisoners rise as visitation ends. Both Cuddy and Ruby pressed their hands against the dull Plexiglas window in union. They eye each other intently for what felt like forever. Cuddy asks, "Ruby, if I say Our Love, what do y-"

" Is unlimited." Ruby beams with joy. "Our love is unlimited," Ruby surprises him by finishing his sentence. Theres a big round of applause from inmates and their visitors. Cuddy disappeared into the back and Ruby joined the attorney and her mother at the end of the corridor. Ruby felt fantastic, and so happy to end this dark season of her life. She was now anxiously waiting for spring.

THEE END

At-Tariq (The Comer by Night)
AKA GHOST

#askaboutghostbooks
#fictionsbestkeptsecret